Uroboros Saga
BOOK ONE

By Arthur Walker

For Lizzy

Then fell on Merlin a great melancholy;
He walk'd with dreams and darkness, and he found
A doom that ever poised itself to fall,
An ever-moaning battle in the mist,
World-war of dying flesh against the life,
Death in all life and lying in all love,
The meanest having power upon the highest,
And the high purpose broken by the worm.

~ Tennyson

CHAPTER 1

Uptown, Port Montaigne - Human Health Services Division of Uroboros Financial

2:05 PM, December 19th, 2199 – Days before shutdown

Dr. Barnes checked his watch. His patient was at least five minutes late, something he thought him incapable. The door swung open a moment later, startling the doctor. He hadn't even heard him come into his secretary's office.

"Nice sign," he said, hooking his thumb back over his shoulder.

"Sorry about that," Dr. Barnes said, gesturing to the couch. "She won a trip to the lunar colony resorts and needed a few days off on short notice. The sign directing people to just come on back is usually more useful than a temp,"

He took off his suit jacket first, laying it across the back as neatly as he could. Then, pulling up the cuffs of his slacks slightly, he sat down. Dr. Barnes pulled out his stylus and slate to start taking notes, pausing to adjust the shades so it was dimmer in the room.

"Kale, what would you like to talk about today?" Dr. Barnes said, pushing his glasses back up his nose.

"God," Kale replied looking over at the book shelf.

"That's a deeper subject than what usually possesses you. I see you've been letting your hair grow. Has HR been after you about that?" Dr. Barnes said, taking a few notes on his slate.

"I met Him. I didn't want to, but it was absolutely necessary," Kale replied, his eyes gliding over the covers of the ancient books on the shelves.

"God?"

"Yes."

"Kale, these meetings are for purposes of maintenance only. If you've had an incident..." Dr. Barnes tapped the slate with the stylus as if to switch from notes to something else.

"I'd been told I look and sometimes act like Him, more than the others. I took it upon myself to emulate His values, see to His agenda," Kale continued, folding his hands neatly on his knees.

"Assuming we're talking about the same person, yes, you look like him I suppose. Do you really consider him to be God?" Dr. Barnes asked, his eyebrow raised slightly with concern.

Kale thought about the question for a moment, his dark eyes turning eerily toward Dr. Barnes, who averted his own gaze. Kale bowed his head slightly and stood up to inspect the books on the shelf more closely.

"Did you get new books?" Kale asked.

"Nope, same as I've always had," Dr. Barnes replied.

Kale nodded slowly then looked back over his shoulder at the doctor.

"If you were me, what would you call Him?" Kale asked.

"I take your point with this view, but do you think that such a belief serves you in any way?" Dr. Barnes questioned, reasserting the couch invite.

Kale shook his head.

"It wasn't about me. I wanted to see His vision of things made manifest. I sought no reward and expected no exaltation. The reward would have been in seeing the task through to fruition. I hoped only to understand as He understands. To see Him as He sees Himself," Kale hissed, passing his fingertips across the spines of the books.

"You said you saw him? What do you mean by that? A vision or..."

Kale laughed, startling Dr. Barnes.

"No. Nothing like that. I really saw Him, stood in the same space as they say, and asked Him a difficult question," Kale said, his cruel smile quickly fading from his face.

"Kale, I think you should submit yourself to a more rigorous examination. There are safeguards that make what you are saying difficult or impossible," Dr. Barnes replied as he wrote nervously.

"Do you? Don't you want to know what I asked Him, and what His reply was?" Kale whispered harshly as he returned to the couch.

"Okay. What did you ask him?" Dr. Barnes asked worriedly.

"I'll paraphrase. I asked Him if He still intended to keep His promise, and to fulfill destiny. He replied by saying He only hoped He could keep from devouring Himself," Kale said sadly, looking up piously.

Dr. Barnes couldn't understand what was happening. He'd sent the signal for armed response minutes ago and no one had arrived yet. He could tell Kale was dangerously unhinged, but didn't understand how he could have done what he claimed.

"What did he look like?" Dr. Barnes asked, stalling for time.

"Oh, He looked as I do, but far more well-traveled and at the same time fearful. It was wretched to see Him that way. I believe that we had both been deceived, and that our meeting was not chance. It had been contrived of a shadowy cabal within my own Maker's institution," Kale said, leaning back on the couch.

"Deceived? Who do you think has deceived you?" Dr. Barnes asked. He looked nervously up toward the door.

"Human Resources, the board of directors, the acting CEO, and you, my good doctor," Kale replied coolly.

Dr. Barnes froze. It seemed impossible that Kale could know the things he knows, let alone say them aloud. There were supposed to be safeguards, things to make what was happening right now impossible. Kale had a low rating, and was considered to have only the most minimal absorption.

"You look surprised, Dr. Barnes," Kale replied, just as though they were discussing the weather.

Dr. Barnes checked his connectivity to the corporate network, but the icon on his slate was gray. Nothing he'd transmitted requesting armed response or Human Resources had gone through for the last ten minutes at least. He decided to play the only card he had.

"Kale, someone is playing you," Dr. Barnes replied calmly. "None of this is real. You couldn't have done what you say you did."

"Oh, I know. I thought I had killed Him at first. In a moment of sheer desperation, feeling more abandoned than I ever have in my very short life, I struck Him down. Like any other man, He bled," Kale said, bowing his head in genuine remorse.

"That can't be. I've seen him recently via our corporate management meetings. His face was right there among all the other directors on the board. You might have hurt someone you thought was him, but it couldn't have happened as you're describing. Let me get you some help," Dr. Barnes said, resuming his professional decorum.

"Have you ever stood in the same room with Him? Seeing His face rendered by so many pixels across a touch screen or the conference glass in the hallway isn't really seeing Him. No, I saw Him, and I struck Him," Kale said, nodding as his eyes grew wide with certitude.

The doctor bolted for the door, but Kale shoved him hard into the bookcase sending many of them to the floor with him. Dr. Barnes turned over grasping for his glasses. Kale grabbed him by his lapels and pushed him back into his chair. Carefully, he put the doctor's glasses back on his face and his slate and stylus back in his hands.

"Where are you going? I've got at least twenty minutes left," Kale asked sardonically.

Unable to bear the sight, Kale began replacing the books on the shelf, exactly where they were, from memory. Dr. Barnes finally caught his breath as Kale placed the last book on the shelf. Kale was faster and stronger than he had right to be, as if something had awakened programming and capabilities that should have been rendered utterly dormant.

"The takeover. You should have been all rendered incapable of this level of awareness," Dr. Barnes muttered breathlessly.

"See, that's what I thought, too. When the rest were demoted or reassigned, I was given something that was so completely opposite my original function. That is when something must have happened. Do you think that the failsafe might itself have a failsafe?" Kale mused as he returned to the couch.

"I'm not afraid of you." Dr. Barnes rubbed his bruised shoulder.

"I've been reading all the sterilized files. I know at least one of my brethren has killed, his quest for the Maker driving him to the brink. At least, that is what anyone with peeking privileges is supposed to think," Kale said shaking his head as if to scold Dr. Barnes.

"It's completely true," Doctor Barnes said with a nod. "One of them did go rogue,"

Kale stood up swiftly covering the distance to where Dr. Barnes sat and leveled a single finger at him, inches from his face. The doctor flinched, holding his hand up defensively. Kale's mouth was agape as if he were about to start screaming, eyes bulging with anger, and no small amount of frustration. Instead, he stood up erect and straightened his tie.

"Let that be the last lie you ever tell me," Kale whispered. "I swear, if you tell another, this conversation will end in a way you'd prefer it didn't."

Dr. Barnes watched wordlessly as he returned to the couch.

"It was a machine, but not in the way that I, or even you, are a machine. I'm virtually indiscernible from you or your secretary for instance. This thing you say has been doing all the killing is a shameful copy of what I am, disparate and primitive," Kale said, his hands moving in the air as if to draw some sort of unseen diagram.

"Okay. What does that have to do with anything?" Dr. Barnes asked, his breath quickening.

Kale laughed, a full and bawdy laugh that filled Barnes with a strange anxiety. Whatever Kale had figured out was clearly above his pay grade and he wasn't sure he wanted to hear the answer now. Kale wiped tears from his eyes with a carefully folded silken hanky fetched from his suit jacket.

"It was all I needed to connect the dots. The takeover, my own mis-information, and the means by which I'd been manipulated. It was hastily done. There were expenses, a trail of paper, and even more than that, there was names and faces and yet more names!" Kale replied, holding his hands out to his sides as if he were giving the doctor a gift.

"These things happen. Finance companies silently take each other over all the time, assets change hands, records are cleansed by the CGG, and the shareholders are none the wiser. It is just business as usual," Dr. Barnes said, trying to calm the situation.

Kale smiled broadly, lips pressed tightly together, cheeks quivering to grant him a sinister countenance.

"It was simple to make your secretary think she'd won a contest. I expensed the whole thing as a means of sweetening a deal with one of my blessedly few shadow clients. Arranging for your office and associated systems to be offline during our conversation was a little more complex, but so far the effort has been utterly worth it," Kale said calmly.

Dr. Barnes smiled weakly, hoping this was all some cruel joke. He set the data slate and stylus down and clasped his hands together. He couldn't pull together everything Kale was saying, but he was certain his normally stable patient had completely lost his mind.

"So, what did you really want to talk about today?" Dr. Barnes asked, his gaze settling on the floor by his feet.

"I wanted to see how much of what was happening beneath the surface of our mutual employer was known to you," Kale replied.

"And?"

"Your body language and every micro-expression seems to suggest that you knew enough to keep your mouth shut, but when pressed to act in the name of our mutual employer's behalf, you took a pay bump instead," Kale stated coldly.

"I didn't take any sort of--"

"Oh, it was all done very well. An adjustment of your credit rating, lifetime debt records, a slight boost to your yearly access of company stock, and expense reports that just got lost somehow. It was probably handled by one of my brothers in every case. It took weeks for me to untangle," Kale said, interrupting the doctor.

"Did you kill him? Is he dead?" he asked.

"No, but He cannot continue His work until He sorts a few things out," Kale replied.

"How do you feel about that?"

"I will simply have to continue His work where I can, subsume corporate resources to that end, and erode the new regime's power until He is well enough to return. I didn't mean to harm Him like that, and I've only an inkling of what I'm capable of. I will atone for what I've done to Him, and there will be those who join me in my endeavor," Kale said, standing up and pulling on his jacket.

"And those who intend to only get in your way," Doctor Barnes said, resigned to his fate.

"Intent implies deliberate thought. In most cases it is those thinking the least deliberately that stand in my way the most. Those who do not question authority and our corporate austerities to the lengths they should. I wanted to see Him as He saw Himself, and until I did, I was utterly blind," Kale said, pulling out his mobile and checking the time.

Kale took Dr. Barnes by the arm and dragged him from the chair. The middle aged man struggled for a moment until Kale could rest his other hand on his head. There was a brief exchange of bio-electric current and Dr. Barnes went completely limp. Kale set him back in his chair and took up his data slate.

He read the doctor's notes with an amused expression for several minutes until he finally deleted them from the device. Laying the slate down on the table beside the unconscious doctor, Kale turned to the book shelf and selected the tome he'd been eyeing for some time.

"Art and the Creative Unconscious. Oh, I can borrow this? Thank you," Kale whispered as he exited the office.

When Dr. Barnes awoke, he had no memory of who he was or how he'd gotten there. He could deduce certain things from the degrees hanging on the wall, the data slate in his hand, and the files in his cabinet, but the rest was a mystery. He could only discern from the pictures on the wall and by gazing for a moment at his reflection that he was part of the psychiatric community.

It occurred to him that it would be particularly bad if any of his colleagues discovered he'd lost his faculties.

CHAPTER 2

Downtown, Port Montaigne – Old Commercial District

11:05 PM, December 17th, 2199

Silverstein's Log, Part 1

I woke up in an unfamiliar and decidedly dirty place, lying on my side, a blurry smudge poking me with a long aluminum baton. A sharp unrelenting headache spread little motes of light across my optical nerve when I blinked. Reaching up I realized that it was more than something you take aspirin for. Someone had hit me. Hard.

My clothes were soaked with rain and sweat. The baton prodded me again, and the smudge stepped in closer. He took shape as he leaned in to look at me, a white guy in his late 40s, his face adorned with a well-trimmed mustache, dressed in a uniform, and a marvelous rain coat, that in my current state, I couldn't help but envy.

"Sir, you can't sleep here," the uniformed man told me insistently.

Sitting up, I looked around at the red brick alley I was lying in, the dingy walls intermittently illuminated by the red and blue flashing lights at the far end. I lifted my hands up to my face and rubbed my fingers together trying to warm them. I couldn't say how long I'd laid there, but I was already covered in a fine coating of grit or soot. The uniformed man helped me to my feet and pressed my hand to the smooth glass of his data slate. It blinked in response, briefly illuminating the uniformed man's face.

"Well, you've got no warrant for your arrest and you aren't registered in the transient report. Sir, I'm going to ask you for ID," the uniformed man stated impatiently.

I couldn't even remember what pocket I kept my wallet. My clothes weren't familiar, and my obvious confusion at my circumstances only elicited a tired glance from the uniformed man as I fumbled about in my pockets. My right rear pocket was turned inside out, whatever I had stored there was now missing. I tried to explain that I didn't have ID, bringing my hand up to my head.

The uniformed man winced as I pushed my hair back searching for the source of the pain.

"Sir, you've got a nasty head wound. There's a clinic nearby. I'll give you a ride," the uniformed man said pulling on some latex gloves.

He helped me toward his transport by the arm. His vehicle marked 'POLICE' in big white letters hummed faintly, the sound muffled by the rain. The blue and white exterior was riddled and pocked with small arms fire. The interior of the pilot's compartment was illuminated by a half dozen monitors each displaying several, from my perspective at least, blurry lines of text. I gestured toward several lines of text that blinked red.

"Woes of the city, my friend," the uniformed man said with a weak smile, helping me into the back of his transport. "You are just one of many calls I get to answer tonight."

The transport rose quickly into the air, passing effortlessly over the traffic below. The lights of the city streamed into the very narrow slits of the passenger compartment. The interior betrayed something of every moment endured by other folks who had also enjoyed the same accommodations. The seats were marred by people wearing restraints, but the floor seemed conspicuously clean. I asked the uniformed man what he did for a living, still hazy and trying awkwardly to just make conversation.

The uniformed man shook his head, my question only betraying more of my dazed and confused state. "I'm a Port Montaigne Police Officer. What do you do, sir?" he half shouted so I could hear him though the polycarbonate shield separating us.

I couldn't remember anything. My name, where I came from, what I did for a living, or why I was lying in an alley all beat to hell. My response was weak, mumbling something about jockeying a desk my whole life trying to take care of the kids. I didn't want a member of Law Enforcement looking at me too closely, in case I was someone who wanted to avoid such attention.

"Tough luck. It's a long shot, but if you could tell me what your wallet looked like, and a description of the guy, or gal, who brained you, that'd help me with my report," the Police Officer replied, routing a report form to a badly scratched touch screen next to where I was sitting.

I filled out the form, giving whatever description came to mind. I hated to prevaricate in case it might help me connect with my identity, but I also couldn't risk unwanted attention with the police. I didn't understand why I would have such an instinct at all. The police officer would probably try to help me if I asked.

"Alright, Mr. Smith. We'll be in contact. We don't come downtown much, so I wouldn't count on us finding what was stolen from you. Weird mobile number, not from around here, huh?"

I assured the officer I'd lived in the Port Montaigne area for a while, keeping my old mobile after I moved. He nodded, only half listening to me as he brought his transport down lower, the lights of the street flooding back into where I was sitting. I looked down at the officer's name as he helped me out of the back of his transport. Collins.

Officer Collins took me by the arm and helped me into the clinic. It was old, still using fluorescent lighting, the archaic aluminum commercial storefront marred and corroded from the ravages of time and what I assumed was nearly constant rainfall. After flashing his badge at the surveillance camera there was an audible click and we were allowed to enter. Officer Collins sat me down in the waiting room in an aged plastic chair.

Curious, I turned and looked at the date stamp on the glass. 2144, the glass was tempered right here in Port Montaigne. I couldn't remember what year it was, but it had to be at least thirty years after the glass had been installed by the dilapidated state of the clinic.

After a few moments an elderly man entered the room wearing a white coat, a battered stethoscope hanging around his neck. I smiled weakly at the antiquated piece of equipment, wondering if I'd seen one outside of a book or old TV show. The brief flash of memory at recognizing the item did little to comfort me as I struggled to fill out the basic medical form put in front of me.

"Took a bad tumble. Lost his wallet," Officer Collins related to the doctor, an elderly man whose name tag betrayed him as one Dr. Helmet.

"A tumble? It looks as though a pipe wandered into your cranium," Dr. Helmet said, wincing at the sight of me.

There were a few ancient magazines languishing in the plastic folders screwed into the walls beside the door. The wallpaper was peeling down slowly from the ceiling, the wages of time evident everywhere in the tan and orange colored clinic. The carpet was of the brown industrial variety, fraying around the threshold at the door.

I didn't have any money to pay for medical attention, and I felt obliged to tell the good doctor I had little I could compensate him with.

"I treat the transient population here. None of you guys have money, but then you aren't a transient are you, Mr. Silverstein?" Dr. Helmet remarked as he inspected my wound.

I looked at him somewhat startled.

"Your shoes. They're hand made in Italy by the Silverstein Company. They even match and fit, not standard issue for transients," Dr. Helmet replied, running a quick CT scan with his handheld.

I nodded looking down at my shoes. Like the rest of what I was wearing I couldn't remember if they were mine, or where I got them. The good doctor frowned looking up from his handheld, running a light across my eyes.

"You've got pretty severe head trauma. I wouldn't be surprised if your vision and motor skills weren't affected for a few weeks, served up with a side of short-term memory loss."

I could only nod numbly, reaching for a magazine. I held it up and waited while Dr. Helmet gave me a local anesthetic. He explained to me that the stitches would dissolve on their own and that I wouldn't have to return unless I exhibited signs of motor control or memory loss. I put on my best smile and asked him where the nearest tourism office was. He looked into my face searching for any sign that I wasn't okay.

"Promise me you'll come back if you display any of the symptoms I described."

I promised, and asked to use his restroom. He nodded and showed me the way to a wheelchair accessible room with a toilet and a sink. The room smelled of disinfectant and the light flickered in time with an odd buzzing sound that preceded a fan beginning to turn in the ceiling.

I closed the door and turned to face the mirror above the sink. I looked like your average white guy, dressed in dirty business casual, short professional haircut, less than a day's worth of stubble on my face. Looking down at my hands, I saw neatly trimmed nails, and no signs of hard labor. I wasn't powerfully built, but probably a runner.

I cleaned myself up as well as I could and straightened my clothing. I washed my hands vigorously, something my muscles seemed to remember. You'd think someone with amnesia would at least remember being an obsessive compulsive, but I wasn't so fortunate. I straightened my hair and stepped back out into the clinic.

I made small talk with Doctor Helmet trying to come off as normal as possible. I assured him I'd send a contribution to the clinic as soon as I got home and thanked him for his help. He handed me my shirt, my hand trembling slightly. It was awkward buttoning up my shirt, taking me a moment to figure out if I was left or right handed. The doctor frowned and shook his head.

"Are you sure you feel well enough? I could send for an ambulance and have you taken to Midtown Medical," Dr. Helmet said, raising an eyebrow.

"I'll be okay," I replied. I signed the release papers with a flourish as "Mr. Mark Smith," then tucked a copy into my pants pocket.

I left the clinic and, using the directions the good doctor gave me, made my way toward the tourism office. Port Montaigne was a large city, huge buildings with hundreds of floors stretching up to the clouds which seemed to continually rain. The ground, even as heavily trafficked as it was, showed signs of moss. I could faintly smell the ocean and breathed it in deeply hoping the scent would jog my memory.

There were transients everywhere in this part of downtown, their creased faces illuminated by the digital bill and reader boards. I kicked at the trash as I continued to walk in my reportedly expensive shoes. The clouds rumbled angrily as it began to rain again. The whole scene seemed familiar, like an old movie maybe. As usual, nothing was coming to me. A blank slate I was.

I marveled at how brilliant the city seemed above the midtown threshold that separated uptown and downtown. The division was striking, and I wondered what someone dressed like me was doing down here. It wasn't that I felt aloof or that I was probably better than anyone living downtown, it was merely the skin I'd woken up in.

The stares I got were proof that someone who appeared as I didn't get down this way much. Uptown and the adjoining concrete and steel supports only blotted out the sky more and more as I went what I was certain to be west. Pretty soon it was just pipes, air conditioning ducts, concrete some fifty feet up, and little else.

The tourism office was a telling place. No merchandise and unmanned, just a somewhat lit space with a few fliers. I grabbed up one and opened it to gaze inside. It bore a 2178 copyright but appeared old. Even aged by time, the printed interior of the flier showed a bright place with a catching graphic of ivory towers presiding over a city of promise and prosperity. The city described in the flier might have been Port Montaigne a long time ago.

I put the flier in my pocket along with a small pencil found lingering in a cup next to the visitors log. I turned to leave as a young woman bounced into the narrow booth next to me. She looked up and smiled weakly brushing the rain from her medium length pink and purple hair.

"Oh sorry, I was just trying to get out of the rain."

I nodded retreating into the booth so she wouldn't have to step back out into the rain to let me out. She smiled and shook her head somewhat bemused and took out a hand rolled cigarette. I watched her light it up, and I breathed deeply of the fragrance of the smoke.

"Most of you guys would just wave their stock picks in my face and shove me back into the rain. You've got all the classic signs, tan lines where there were rings on your fingers, obscenely expensive shoes, and that manicure? What's an up-towner like you doing downtown anyway?"

"Us guys?"

"High-rise corporate types."

I nodded smiling for a moment remembering how I looked, and the way I was dressed. I looked down at my hand, she was right, it looked like I might have been wearing at least one ring. She continued to look up at me somewhat confused.

She was young, but it was clear she'd already seen the darkest places of the world. Her brightly colored outfit had been cobbled together, probably hand sewn, her tattoos were cheap but well thought out. She was meticulous about her appearance and I could see she carried her own soap when she put her lighter back in her colorful handbag.

"I'm not a prostitute."

"I didn't think you were. You'd have sensed by now I don't have any money, or interest, and moved on."

"Then why are you still talking to me?"

"The soap. I obsessively wash my hands too, always nice to meet someone with a similar hang up."

"I wash dishes at the Strip and Waffle, but that's all I do there."

"I believe you. Too short to be a dancer."

She slugged me playfully.

"I'm Taylor."

"Silverstein."

"Like the shoes?"

"Yeah, like the shoes."

We shook hands. I wondered why a girl her age wasn't in college. Why her parents weren't doing everything they could to give her a better life than living in downtown Port Montaigne. I wondered why I even wondered about such things.

"I have to work my shift, it'll be breakfast time soon. Split a waffle with me?"

I nodded and followed her back out into the crowded streets, the rain having slowed somewhat. She wove her way through the crowd, nimbly avoiding the grasping hands of transients and the wandering eyes of pimps and what were probably worse. Why she wanted me, a total stranger to walk with her, suddenly made sense. I walked along beside her like I was her father, occasionally pointing to an obscure landmark and made small talk. I held her hand as we crossed the street doing my best to keep up the act.

There were other folks walking the darkened and sky deprived streets of downtown as well. There were preachers, dock workers, and a healthy number of rickshaws being peddled from one place to another. It was all lit with old neon lighting, dilapidated Christmas lights, and barrel fires shrouded by folks trying to warm their hands.

It was noisy, too. I could hear a dozen different languages being spoken at any given time and there was every sort of person under the sun, not that one could actually see the sun. The only thing any of them seemed to have in common was whatever business it was that kept them from midtown or uptown. To the east, one could see the divisions between districts more clearly, with midtown rising up to meet the port and then to what little I could see of the bowels of uptown.

When we arrived at the Strip and Waffle, we ducked through the side door. The back room was crowded with cans of peaches and bags of pancake powder. It was a wonderful if somewhat unfamiliar smell. I walked past the dressing rooms averting my eyes as I followed her. She turned and looked back at me smiling.

"I was sure you were a total perv."

"Disappointed?"

"Nope, you can keep pretending to be my daddy all you want," she said, her face almost glowing in the dark of the back room when she smiled.

"It's nice to be wanted."

Taylor led me back into the cleanest place I could remember. At the center of the kitchen stood a dark skinned man, Mediterranean by his accent. He smiled at Taylor and extended his hand in greeting.

"I'm Joe."

"Silverstein. I'm pretending to be Taylor's dad tonight."

"She usually takes a cab, but I think she's been saving her tips for something."

Taylor only rolled her eyes and looked over at me, her face apologetic.

"I promised you a waffle."

"It's okay, maybe some other time."

I turned and followed Joe out. As we passed by his office I could see mountains of printed documents littering the desk. My hackles went up at the sight and I paused, my gaze lingering on the pile of unpaid notices, invoices, and vouchers.

"Yeah, it's a terrible mess. I run a good club, best waffles in town, but I'm no bookkeeper."

"Mind if I take a look?"

"You want me to let a total stranger look at my financials because he walked my dishwasher to work?"

"Yes."

"Hey, knock yourself out."

Joe wandered back to the kitchen throwing his hands into the air in disbelief. I sat down at his desk, and began rapidly sorting the paper work. My mind, while entirely incapable of remembering anything about myself, quickly dissected the financial documents spread across Joe's desk.

What became clear was that Joe was making money, but paying too much in taxes by not keeping good records and making the right claims. A few of the dancers brought me a plate of waffles and a cup of coffee while I worked. Each gave me a strange look and a smile, lingering in the event I wanted to make small talk. I didn't.

For some reason I could not resist the urge to create order in Joe's office. From the dates on the most recent invoices it was sometime in December, 2199. The accounting wizardry I seemed to possess came easily once I began looking at the numbers, receivables, and invoices. It was good to feel a measure of control, and that I at least had a skill. A few hours of work would net Joe a tidy return from overpaid taxes, and show that at least one of his suppliers was overcharging.

Hours later, rubbing his eyes sleepily, Joe walked by his office as I was putting the finishing touches on his books. He stepped in, mouth agape for a moment. He failed to hide his expression that was one part relief and two parts appreciation.

"Mr. Silverstein, you really didn't have to do this."

"It's just Silverstein. The government and one of your suppliers owe you some money. I'd file as soon as you can, there's a limitation on how long you can wait before the money is irrecoverable."

"That supplier. He's overpaid on purpose."

"Tip?"

"Protection. You're definitely not from around here."

"No."

I stood up, reaching behind me for a coat that wasn't there. I squinted trying to remember the source of the gesture. That kind of muscle memory or reflex seemed to indicate that I always had a jacket or a coat. Where the hell was my coat?

"You okay, Silverstein?"

"No."

"Look, I owe you, and I don't get the feeling you're here to shake me down. What can I do for you?"

"The coffee and waffles were really good."

"Yeah, the girls did that. Can I buy you cab home?"

"I have nowhere to go."

"Guy like you? You in some kind of trouble?"

"I can't go home until I figure some things out."

Joe nodded. He seemed to genuinely understand my plight somehow, without knowing the details. Putting his hands in his pockets he pulled out a wad of cash and placed it on the desk in front of me.

"That's three hundred. It'll at least give you something to travel with."

"I think I'll be staying close. Hard to find a good waffle."

"Anytime you want waffles, just sit down at my desk and work your magic. All you can eat."

I nodded shaking Joe's hand. Taylor came by and gazed in at us with a strange smile crossing her face. She looked about the office in wonderment, her eyes wide with mock surprise.

"It's the apocalypse! Joe's desk is clean!"

"Hey, I pay you to wash dishes not comment on my decor. You outta get home now Taylor, it's late."

"Okay, Joe. You gonna walk me home, Silverstein?"

I nodded, waving goodbye to Joe. I followed Taylor through the back room and out the side door into the alley. It was almost noon, but you couldn't tell by looking around outside. The tangle of concrete and utility housings that held uptown aloft completely blotted out the sky here. Not a single shaft of sunlight touched the ground.

Taylor grabbed my hand as we again traveled through the streets as though we were father and daughter. It was a comfortable facade, even if completely unfamiliar. If there was a silver lining about not being able to remember anything, it is that everything seems new. The rain on my face, the touch of a young girl's hand, and every smell and sensation was novel and unfamiliar.

We warmed ourselves by a barrel fire, and after turning down several offers to trade for my shoes, we headed to what Taylor called The Commons. The building sat as though it were squatting beneath the huge metropolitan murk above us, drooping at the corners like a clown with no one to perform for. The outside had once been yellow with a red commercial facade out front.

There was no doorman, but she did have to enter a code. Obviously, this wasn't somewhere people just hid from the rain. There was a landlord, paying tenants, and warmth. The furnace seemed to work nicely. Taylor stopped in the lobby, turning her gaze back toward me.

"I left my mobile charging up in my room. Want me to call you cab a somewhere?"

"I have nowhere to go. Is there somewhere nearby they'd just let me crash?"

"You can't go home?"

"No."

Taylor seemed to stop and think for a moment before stepping uncomfortably close to me.

"Silverstein, do you like me? I mean, is there any chance that--"

"No."

She looked hurt at first but then broke into a wide grin.

"You really aren't a pervert?"

"Taylor, I honestly can't recall if I am or not."

She looked at me somewhat bewildered, then smirked as I pointed at the stitches on my head. She laughed out loud, a real, honest to God laugh that ended with her clapping her hands together once. I smiled sleepily, my head started to pound. I could see her eyes grow wide for a moment as I pitched forward. I came to rest roughly in front of her, my crumpled form too weak to rise.

"You better not be faking it, old man."

Taylor grabbed me around the chest and dragged me to the elevator. My vision swam with black and red as my head continued to pound mercilessly. I shut my eyes as the elevator doors closed trying to blot out the terrible music playing in the background. After taking a few moments to rest in the hallway, Taylor dragged me the rest of the way to her room.

"Nice place."

She looked down at me and frowned as she dragged me through beaded curtains across what felt like every sharp or uncomfortable thing one could possibly think to leave strewn about on the floor. She laid me down and looked me over.

The walls were painted in thousands of colors, and she had a rather impressive wardrobe arrayed across the walls. I wasn't sure they weren't all hallucinations until I saw the ancient sewing machine and mounds of cloth. She was some kind of artist, probably the one that made the clothing she was wearing.

"Silverstein, you're as white as a sheet and your eyes. They--"

"Shock... maybe... get me a blanket, please."

She wandered over and draped a multicolored quilt over the top of me, and tried to give me some water from a clay mug she likely sculpted herself.

"Is there anything in here you didn't make?"

"Please don't talk. You're really in a bad way. I should call a doctor."

"No, please. Taylor, I don't know who I am."

"So what?"

"What if I'm a bean counter for the mob, a wanted man, or a witness under government protection?"

"That would be awesome! Probably get a reward for turning you in."

"Or you could get hurt or mixed up in whatever trouble I'm in."

Taylor smiled down at me. Maybe it was the concussion, but again, there was almost a radiance that issued forth when she smiled like that.

"What?"

"You don't even know me, Silverstein. You'd die on my floor before letting something bad happen to me?"

"Yeah, I think I would. You're my only friend."

"Oh, so we're friends now are we?" Taylor said shaking her head and smirking.

Taylor took a deep breath and gathered a stack of wet wash cloths and kept me cool through the afternoon and probably past dinner time, I couldn't be sure. While I was blacked out she must have kept a vigil next to me, because she was there sleeping when I awoke. It was dark outside now, and I felt terrible for being such an inconvenience to her. She woke with a start, her face quickly overcome with relief.

"I thought you'd never wake up."

"My head still hurts a little, I think I overdid it yesterday."

"Well, take it easy today then. You can stay here with me until you're better. I guess. Unless you piss me off or touch me."

"No deal."

"What?"

"Taylor, I don't know who I am. I could be some guy who got mugged, has a regular job, and a family, or I could be someone mixed up in something dangerous."

Taylor displayed a pained expression then looked down at the floor, her pink and purple hair obscuring her face for a moment. I tried to sit up but the pain in my head was so intense I had to sit right back down. I didn't want to stay and cause her any more havoc than I already had, but it was looking like I didn't have a choice.

"Silverstein, you aren't going anywhere. That someone didn't roll you for black market donor organs already is nothing short of a miracle in your condition. You shouldn't go anywhere."

"Then help me blend in."

"What do you mean?"

"My shoes, what do you think they'd sell for?"

"Nine hundred easy," Taylor replied, affirming what I already suspected.

"There's another three hundred in my pocket. Sell my shoes, and as soon as I can get up we'll go clothes shopping. By then I should have a beard. Assure Joe I'll be in to look at his books again when I'm better."

"You want me to play dress up with a man twice my age so he can hide from dangerous people that may or may not exist?"

"Bad idea?"

"Awesome idea! Gay or straight?"

"What?"

"How do you want to dress?"

"Straight. It'll be easier for me to pose as your father that way."

"What year do you think it is? No one thinks that way anymore."

"Where are your parents anyway?" I asked, not seeing any family photos or other mementos about her apartment.

"I'm twenty-one."

"Look, I don't remember a thing, so I can't break the ice by offering up a tidbit about myself."

"Really? You got mugged, conked on the head, and now you can't remember who you are?"

"Yes."

"I thought you were just handing me some lame-o story down in the lobby. So dumb. That's why I laughed."

"Cliche or not, it's the truth."

Taylor looked incredulous for a moment but seemed to resolve to give me the benefit of the doubt for the moment.

"Would I let you sell my shoes if I was lying and planning to just bail the first opportunity I got?"

"Depends. How many Silversteins do you own, Silverstein?"

"Would you sell your shoes if it wasn't a real emergency?"

"No, but it is different for guys."

"Oh no, I might not remember who I am, but I must have been a serious shoe guy to have forked out for even a single pair of these."

Taylor pulled out her mobile, noted the time, and headed for the door.

"I liked you better unconscious, and DON'T go organizing my apartment while I'm out. I WILL kill you."

I nodded weakly lying back down. Taylor stood and went out for what I could only guess was thirty minutes. She opened some fragrant takeout she'd procured somewhere nearby and began lifting it to my mouth deftly with a pair of chopsticks. Satisfied I'd had enough to eat she went into the next room and grabbed a large stuffed bear and stuck it under my head.

"Aren't you going to miss him?"

"I have a backup."

Taylor winked stepping into the tiny bathroom closing the door behind her. She showered, washed her hands vigorously, and then reemerged in a set of bulky purple leopard print pajamas. She knelt down and gazed at me intently as she finished off the remainder of the takeout.

"Silverstein, do you think we'll still be friends after you remember who you are?"

"I'm sure. You really think I'll get my memory back?"

"Do you really think the objective medical opinion of a dishwasher at a strip joint counts?"

"Yes."

"I think you'll eventually remember who you are. We might be able to find out if you register as a transient or you have a record."

"No good. I was already picked up by one of Port Montaigne's finest. I'm not in the system."

"And the Citizen's Privacy Act prevents him looking you up or identifying you until a missing persons report is filed."

"Right."

"You really care what I think?"

"Yeah. I believe that if you have a friend pulling for you, the universe takes that into account relative to how things go down."

"When did you start believing that?"

"About five minutes ago."

"Convenient."

"You and a small shred of hope are all I have right now, Taylor. I'm scared, not just for me, but for you, too. I'm not even sure why."

"You think the normal instinct for someone in your position would be to assume they're a normal person conked on the head?"

"Yeah."

"However, because you can't reconcile being an average Joe, your instinct is that you're in some kind of trouble."

"Correct."

Taylor picked up her mobile and snapped a picture of me. She turned the screen toward her, her fingers gliding across the touchscreen.

"What are you doing?"

"I'm going to see if a missing persons report has been filed yet."

"Probably not yet. Might not have been long enough to allow someone to file. I don't know how long the police make a person wait before they can declare someone missing."

"I'll keep looking. Try to rest, Silverstein."

"That's a nice mobile, where'd you get it?"

"Bought it with tip money, it's the only one I've owned that I haven't lost."

I nodded weakly, my insides knotted up from the anxiety I felt. What if I was a wanted fugitive, or a rapist, or someone who would hurt Taylor upon recovering his memory? I had to believe I wasn't a horrible person. That in the wake of forgetting who I was, I would garner the power to change for the better.

"Taylor, ever fantasize about falling asleep and waking up as someone completely different?"

"Sometimes."

"Take it from someone who knows, be glad you are who you know yourself to be. Revel in every moment you live your life with a known identity."

"I'm a dishwasher at a strip club."

"No. You're an artist, and a good one. This apartment is filled with nothing but things made from your own hands. It's beautiful, and while I can't remember much, there's no place I'd rather be laid up. Whatever my life was before, getting hit on the head was worth the chance to see your works. Please, show me some more of your stuff."

Taylor smiled, her eyes glistening slightly. She leapt up and grabbed item after wondrous item from her apartment. This girl was truly a diamond in the rough. She had taken the rare scrap of color found in the gray dingy streets below and brought it up to her apartment to be made into something beautiful.

In truth, she'd done the same with me. I was something that obviously didn't belong in the downtown of Port Montaigne, and through a strange twist of fate, I found myself along her path. Like everything else in her apartment, I was brought here tattered, then made whole by her hands.

"Taylor."

"Yeah?"

She looked down at me over a garment that she'd just put the finishing touched on. It was a marvelous creation that must have taken her months to collect the materials for. I could tell she was proud of it, the sequins lovingly stitched glittering in her excited eyes. I looked at the garment, then up at her, and uttered the only words that seemed to make sense.

"I won't let anything happen to you. I promise."

CHAPTER 3

Downtown, Port Montaigne - Peddler's District

2:37 PM, December 20th, 2199

Silverstein's Log, Part 2

I wasn't back on my feet an hour before Taylor was dragging me, and her largest bag, to something she called the Peddler's District. According to the flier I nabbed from the Tourism Booth, there were several huge concrete malls and attractions being constructed by the seaside. They were to be concrete forms, mass manufactured to have shops, condominiums, and manufacturing facilities installed easily. Apparently none of that panned out.

In the place where those attractions were to have been built, the Peddlers District sprang up instead. It's a twenty-four hour flea market where one can procure anything produced downtown, a few things from midtown, and the odd item from uptown. There were thousands of people, each carrying a pack or pushing a cart of goods fighting for space and customers every hour of every day. Taylor navigated it like a fashion-seeking missile, sometimes playfully shoving vendors and patrons aside in a mad dash for what she wanted.

Everyone else appeared to be physically polite but they did their best to thrust their goods in the face of anyone who didn't appear to be a vendor. Under every overpass, within every tunnel, and squatting in the half-finished commercial storefront, there were people. There were all kinds down here, trying to simply survive beneath the shining uptown that seemed to have forgotten them.

There was a triage tent, a couple of makeshift libraries, and folks charging for access to electricity so one could charge their mobile or make use of a toaster. Even fettered by profound amnesia the sight affected me deeply. I wondered if the world I'd forgotten was worth remembering if it had left so many people destitute.

I trailed behind taking in the sights while trying to protect my pockets from sticky fingers. As many vendors as there were, there was at least half that many children squirming their way past in the crowd. Some carried packages for delivery, others were empty handed and looking for a handout.

"I know a gal who will buy your shoes. Then we can get you a full spread to wear for a while."

"I can't wait," I replied sullenly.

"Stop sounding so excited," she scolded, her voice trailing off as the linen section of the district and all its glittering splendor came into view.

The fully contained concrete labyrinth was gloomy except for a few emergency lamps and strings of holiday lights venders had arrayed across their carts and attached to old car batteries. Windows were never cut into the sides of the concrete forms, so one could only hear the sea as opposed to seeing it. The whole of the place was a tapestry for graffiti artists, every wall covered in murals and bright colors.

The Peddler's Market would have been a very drab and depressing place without the artwork that adorned most every wall and pipe. To a trained eye it probably related the lay of the land, social boundaries, and turf held by various underground organizations. To my own eyes, conveying the sight to a mind with no memories, it was an expression of hope and fear, a pair of emotions more interrelated than I was willing to admit at the time.

"Let me borrow your mobile for a moment," I asked her.

"Don't make any long distance calls," she said handing it to me.

I held it up and activated the touch screen so I could look at some of the murals obscured by darkness as we walked along. I felt a bit like an archaeologist unearthing ancient cave paintings. Some of the work was pretty good and very political with regard to the segregation of rich and poor in Port Montaigne.

The most striking was a depiction of a shining city built like a ground stopper to keep what was below from bubbling up. In that crevasse beneath was a multitude of peoples toiling to escape some sort of terrible oppression at the hands of shadowy individuals in rubber suits wielding shock batons and shields. Above it all was a machine, its mechanical tendrils reaching down through it all slowly transforming into pipes and concrete the lower in the mural it got.

Barter seemed to be the primary means of making a transaction as few of these poor souls had currency. Nevertheless, among the hundreds of merchants jostling for space here, I could hear and smell money, and lots of it. I could tell that several shadowy hands were at work behind the scenes, laundering and moving massive amounts of currency through this place unseen.

Taylor's shoe guy, wasn't a guy in any way, except perhaps anatomically. She eventually got argued down to eight hundred thirty seven for my shoes which seemed a bargain relative to the price of most everything else in the district. Proceeds safely in hand, Taylor began going through all the shoes looking for my next pair of footwear. As I watched the merchants wander by, it was as though I could see the numbers and values of everything they were selling floating by with them. In seconds I could easily advise any of these merchants on how to maximize their profit while minimizing their cost.

"What are you staring at?"

"Numbers, Taylor. Just numbers."

"I don't see anything."

"Yes, you do. You see colors, textures, and the means to combine them into something pleasing. So much better than numbers."

She smiled reflexively, but immediately swallowed it, returning to the calm expression she generally put on display while we wandered the streets. It took me a day or so to figure out why, but she didn't dare show anyone her smile. The more I traveled the downtown, the more evident that the smile was a sign of weakness, naivety, or being an outsider. Worse, the people that seemed allowed to smile were always well dressed, and widely feared.

Snapping on a pair of latex gloves, Taylor acquired a pair of canvas slip-ons. She sprayed them with disinfectant while inspecting the interior of them and the laces.

"There isn't a single place to wash your hands in this district, Silver-stein." Taylor said, offering me my own pair of latex gloves.

I nodded grimly, taking a pair of the gloves so I could handle the merchandise.

"I am certain I've never worn a pair of shoes like these before. Likely for very good reason."

"You don't remember anything. How do you know?"

"My feet know."

"They're tough and totally disposable."

"White? They'll be dingy and awful walking around here."

"I am going to dye them for you, and they can be thrown in the laun-dry. That's something you would never do with your Silverstein kicks."

"It's as if all my apprehensions and fears about this footwear have evaporated."

Taylor smirked, then set about selecting several white pairs of the can-vas slip-ons. I paid for them while she slipped them into her enormous bag, her eyes darted about like a hungry predator for more bargains. I swal-lowed nervously as I was dragged towards a cart of garish jackets. She seemed to enjoy my awkwardness a little too much as she made me try on a never-ending array of tasteless jackets, promising that they'd be perfect after a few alterations.

"I like this one," I said turning up the collars of a brown leather jacket.

"Perfect, if you're trying out for Captain Boring's sidekick."

"Ouch."

"This one is the one."

She was right. While garish, it fit me perfectly. She promised to sew on some patches and such to make it more my style. I confessed having no recollection of what my style was. She assured me it would have pouches for my prostate pills and a built-in pocket protector. All things considered, I was relieved to have someone who could take what I'd lost seriously, but still have a sense of humor about it.

"If there is anything I'm sure about, it's that I had a righteous jacket before all this happened. It went everywhere with me. I even reached for it when I stood up from Joe's desk out of habit."

"The jacket I'm going to make for you, will make you forget all about your old one. That is, if you hadn't already forgotten about it."

She laughed. Not defensively, but a genuine laugh. I could tell it had been a while since she'd been really happy, or that anyone had made her feel important or appreciated. I was happy, too. Glad to just have a friend. I wondered if I had someone who was as good a companion in life as Taylor before I lost my memory. I paused to wonder if that person was looking for me.

"Look at these shirts! Aren't these great?!"

"Those, yes. Those... um, no."

"You don't know who you will be tomorrow. You should always have some color to spare just in case you stop being blue and start being red."

"Good point. Let's get them all."

Taylor smiled as I forked over what little I had left for the shirts, a few pairs of pants, and more socks than I could possibly wear in a whole year. I gazed at the large bag she brought with her, which now bulged with clothing, slip-on shoes, and one special jacket. It would all become my identity for now, until I could figure out who I was. My slip-on identity, easily granted color, easily laundered.

We wandered back through the Peddler's District, taking turns carrying the bag full clothes. Having made several purchases, the vendors seemed to grant us some measure of respect. As we approached them, they wouldn't target us specifically with their pitches and seemed to step aside to allow us passage; a barely audible showing of appreciation.

The quiet dignity of the people who lived in and did business here was a stark contrast to one's first impression. They were dirty, loud, but they knew how to treat the customer in the aftermath of an honest purchase. Even if I couldn't respect their attention to hygiene, I could respect their reverence for others who worshiped the holy practice of commerce.

As we reached the outskirts of the district I could see several men and women walking together. Each was dressed in a black rubbery suit and carrying a sidearm. They displayed no badge or tag of office, but they appeared to be collecting taxes from the vendors. They were like what I'd seen earlier as part of the mural.

"Taylor, who are those people?"

"Collectors. Everyone pays them for protection downtown."

"Protection from what?"

"People who don't pay get hurt."

"Do you pay?"

"No, but I'm sure Joe does."

I paused to watch for a moment, taking in everything I could see about the collectors. Each had good computer skills, good teeth, and expressed a certain level of disdain for the vendors. They weren't from the downtown area, which meant whoever they worked for wasn't either. For all I had seen of these people, whatever flaws they may have, they didn't deserve being extorted like this.

For the first time I could recall, I was a little angry.

I was glad to step into the open air at last. The rain coming down from what little sky shown through from above seemed to wash the grime of the Peddler's Market off my face. It wasn't to last as the bulwark between uptown and downtown got progressively more intrusive as we walked west. We were thirsty, so Taylor began leading us toward the only place she knew that sold bottled water.

It was a crumbling building that managed to still have power at the edge of the strip where Joe's club and a handful of other establishments were located. Taylor opened the door and promptly slipped backward into my arms. Between her and the weight of the bag I was carrying we went all the way to the ground.

Somewhere in the process of untangling ourselves, I gazed into the corner store and saw what it was Taylor slipped on. Blood had pooled at the threshold, running across the floor from someone laying atop the sales counter. I grabbed Taylor and led her quickly to the other side of the street.

"What? What's wrong?" Taylor asked trying to look past me.

"Wait here, I'll get the water," I said, setting the bag down on the curb beside her.

I walked back over and stepped inside over the pool of blood. The place smelled like a musty store overwrought by terror tinged with iron. It was a horrific sight, arterial blood spatter arraying the wall in crimson beneath a slowly swaying fluorescent light. I looked down at the area immediately around the counter and could see two sets of foot prints.

Squatting I looked at who I assumed was the shop keeper. One set of bloody prints were his, the set that was dragged across the counter while he bled profusely. The other set were unmistakable, almost one of a kind.

I didn't even have to put my own foot down beside one to know exactly what they were, Silverstein brand leather shoes, and same size as mine.

I grabbed two bottles of water and turned toward the door. Taylor was standing there looking inside at me. She was pale with fright, eyes transfixed what little of the shopkeeper was visible from her vantage. At that moment it struck me how likely it was that the killer was still nearby.

"Whoever did this could be close, we should get out of here," I said grabbing her hand.

She gripped my hand tightly and traded me the bag for a bottled water. We moved quickly for several minutes until she tugged at my hand. I stopped, already knowing what she was going to ask.

"Where are we going?" Taylor asked. "My apartment is the other way."

"I want to go to the alley where that police officer found me."

"Do you think it will help you remember?"

"I don't know."

"Why now all of a sudden?"

I took a deep breath.

"I'm pretty sure what happened at the corner store has something to do with me. The killer was wearing my shoes, or shoes like them," I replied.

"Someone must have bought them at the market after we sold them, and went there to rob the place. They aren't cheap after all," Taylor replied, still not understanding.

"I don't know anything about it, but it seemed too brutal for a robbery. Also, the register was untouched and it doesn't look like anything was taken," I replied.

"You don't think it's a coincidence?" she asked.

"How many people with shoes like mine or the money to buy them have you seen down here?" I retorted.

"Just you. Fine," she replied after a moment's consideration. "Let's go look at the alley."

We plodded along, the bag beginning to get heavy from the rain. We took turns carrying it until we arrived at the alleyway. Something seemed terribly wrong as I gazed into that narrow space between the buildings. It was dirty, but not quite dirty enough.

"There should be some blood still here. I had a head wound."

"Unless this isn't where you were attacked."

"Taylor, look at the walls, the dumpsters, and the ground."

"Everything looks scrubbed, or new. Even with a week's worth of the falling soot from uptown, this is a relatively clean alley. This is a terrifying amount of cover up to keep a mugging off the radar."

Taylor stepped in front of me, delivering a savage poke to my belly. She then folded her arms and turned back toward the streets. I couldn't blame her for being angry. It was as I feared, something from my forgotten past had followed me down here. I shifted the bag from one arm to the other as a new weight seemed to fall on my shoulders.

Taylor looked back at me, her face streaked in black, her makeup ruined.

"Silverstein, what are we going to do?"

"I don't know. I don't know anything."

Taylor knelt down beside me holding the lit touchscreen from her mobile under my chin. Even in the rain its dim illumination was enough for her to see my face clearly. Her mouth parted someone surprised as she ran her hands through my hair.

"What?"

"Silverstein, your face…"

I walked over to a wrecked commercial transport and stood in front of its one remaining side view mirror. The gray in my hair was slowly oozing down my face, which seemed suddenly devoid of wrinkles, the rain washing twenty years from my visage. My mind reeled for a moment as my fractured psyche did it's best to piece together what I was seeing.

"I need to get to the clinic," I said.

I broke into a run feeling a strange, almost youthful strength flooding my limbs. Even the rain-soaked bag of clothes did little so slow me down.

"What? Wait up!" Taylor called out after me.

Taylor plodded along effortlessly beside me as we navigated the underground labyrinth of streets toward where the transient population squatted. I was frantic to learn anything about myself at this point.

We breathlessly turned the last corner toward the clinic spotting Dr. Helmet standing outside. He was just locking up, and turned to face me as

I approached. His face filled with bewilderment when he saw me. I nodded to him in greeting raising my hand.

"Dr. Helmet, I need your help."

"Let's go inside," he muttered, shakily unlocking the door.

The doctor ushered me into a back room, where he snapped on the light and offered me a seat on a padded examination table. He wordlessly took a drop of saliva and ran some tests while Taylor gazed inside the ancient fashion magazines in the waiting room. After a few moments, he looked at the test results on his handheld and brought up the previous scans from the night I was attacked.

"Mr. Silverstein, I take it you're experiencing some memory loss?"

"From the head wound? Yes, tell me something I don't know. Please."

"Now that the swelling has gone down, I can see where you might have had some short term memory loss, but nothing like the amnesia you're experiencing right now," Dr. Helmet said, looking at the chart on his handheld.

"Is it that obvious?" I asked.

"I don't get very many folks from uptown who hit me up for treatment. This is just a guess, but you may have been subjected to several chemical treatments that would be extremely difficult to detect with a cursory medical examination. I can't seem to detect any of the usual chemicals one uses to accomplish this however, but I'm somewhat limited down here."

"Accomplish what? You mean something to make me look old, like the temporary treatments to my hair."

"All would have been permanent in death and virtually undetectable. It would have made identifying your body difficult."

"So someone did this to me to make me look old so they could kill me and my body would be unidentifiable?"

"Unlikely. There are better ways to make a body unidentifiable and you would have had to be subjected to these chemicals over a period of time."

"I don't understand."

"If you did this to yourself, the chemical cocktail would have painfully pinched the nerves in your muscles, granting you the appearance of someone much older. Did you experience any pain?"

"Other than the head wound, not at all. How old am I really?"

"From your bone structure, only four or five years older than the young lady in the waiting room. This is just a cursory examination and--"

"How can I discover who I am?" I interrupted.

"There is no legal way to find that out, the CGG voraciously protects the privacy of the citizenry. Only you can access or give permission to access government held medical or personal records, which requires you knowing who you are, or finding someone who does."

"There are people down here that could get me that information illegally?"

"Indeed. These aren't people to be trifled with, Mr. Silverstein. Hacking a government database looking for personal information with only a face and a fingerprint to work with might be pretty difficult."

"What kind of people, Dr. Helmet?"

"Uptown people, like the ones who collect from, provide protection for, the various vendors and businesses downtown."

"Had a few things I been wanting to ask them anyway."

"You sure you want to find out who you are?"

"Wouldn't you?"

"I've a host of things I'd prefer to have forgotten. Whatever you left behind, Mr. Silverstein, it might be best forgotten," the doctor replied with some certitude.

He had a point. I slid off the examination table and back into my new shoes. I buttoned up my shirt and donned my, as yet unaltered, jacket and stepped into the waiting room. Taylor stuffed the magazines beneath her own jacket and looked at the time on her mobile.

"Can we please go home?"

"Home?"

"My apartment."

"Right."

She looked at me impatiently. I nodded grabbing up the wet bag of clothes putting it up to my shoulder. We walked back outside into the dingy street as people began filtering back out, the rain slowing to a trickle.

Taylor walked along in front of me, her arms folded. "Gonna be hard to pose as my dad now."

"You don't like the new me?" I said, flashing a cheesy smile.

"I don't understand something. You come to me, an old man, you even felt old and sounded old."

"None of which can I explain, except to say I genuinely thought I was old," I stated while briefly considering the impact our personal appearance really has on our identity. "I'm sorry. I never meant to deceive you, and I meant what I said."

"About what?" Taylor replied, gazing back at me with tired eyes.

"I won't let anything happen to you."

Taylor's anger melted away quickly as she looked back over her shoulder at me. I could see she was genuinely concerned about all this, and the fact I'd gone to such great lengths to conceal my identity did nothing to assuage my own anxiety, either. Who I was could seriously mess with who I was trying to be.

Regardless, looking at Taylor made me want to be a good person. I had already resolved to be one of the good guys. It didn't matter who I was before, I would make this right to Taylor somehow. In spite of everything going on downtown, she had made a life for herself here and shared the best parts of it with me. I felt a reverence for anything that managed to thrive in that sort of adversity.

The walk back was quiet until we reached the lobby. The landlord awaited us with folded arms. He was a large middle-aged man, with gray working its way through his straight hair. His blue bib overalls were oily, and his gloved hands clenching a wrench.

"Taylor, I understand you've got an unreported roomie."

"Mr. Swenson, this is my da...um, cousin. He's just visiting."

"Yeah, right," the superintendent said casting his gaze in my direction.

I stepped forward and cleared my throat. The old landlord gave me the up and down look, then sneered, obviously not buying the cover story. I swallowed and smiled weakly.

"Mr. Swenson, my name is Silverstein."

The big man only glared at my outstretched hand.

"I'm doing the books over at Joe's Strip and Waffle, is there something along those lines I could for you?"

"I got books, but they don't need keeping. What I need is someone who is willing to get dirty and maybe even hurt going down to fix the furnace. You want your pretty young friend's apartment to stay heated? I need someone willing to help me turn a wrench in the tunnels below."

"Two man job?" I asked.

"Two and a half. You and what little you'll likely bring to the table ought to be enough," Mr. Swenson said glowering downward like he could see through the floor to the misbehaving furnace below.

He shoved a tool box into my arms and beckoned for me to follow. I nodded quietly looking over at Taylor. She took the bag of clothes from me and smiled broadly.

"I'll get these clothes dried up and prepped to be altered while you're down getting your hands all dirty."

"Should I be bothered that you seem to delight in my suffering?" I said, tired enough now that I was just running on adrenaline.

"Think what you want, I'm going to wash my hands."

"Right."

Sighing loudly, I turned to face Mr. Swenson. He squinted menacingly at me at first, then clapped me on the shoulder. The toolbox weighed a ton, and I had to wonder if the old landlord added a few rocks to it for his personal amusement.

We walked through his clean and tidy building to the underground access without a word. I looked around at the doors, steam pipes, stairs, floors, and ceilings likely mended by Mr. Swenson. This whole building was his well-kept kingdom and I'd been asked to walk beside him, an honor of sorts, or just initiation for everyone that stayed there.

You pitched in or got thrown out.

"Did she set this up?"

"Sort of. I asked her if she knew anyone she trusted to help out down below."

"She trusts me?"

"Evidently she does, Mr. Silverstein. You'd be wise to grant that some respect as trust doesn't come cheap down here."

A heavy burden, and likely one she'd bestowed upon me before the events of the day we'd just spent together. Even as I pondered this, I reached down and grabbed the other side of a heavy lid to descend down into a dark place with a man I just met.

"By the way, just call me Silverstein."

"Alright then, call me Russ."

Taking the heavy gauge steel ladder down into the darkness, Russ led me to a small prep room where he had waders and some old helmets rigged with illuminators. There were movie posters, handbills, framed artwork and all manner of decorations adorning the walls down here.

"Taylor?" I asked, pointing to the walls.

"When she was little, she wandered in down here from somewhere and took up residence. Back in those days, I had a building full of paying tenants, so I let her live in here until something freed up. She saved her money and helped out around here," Russ replied, some of his gruff exterior smoothing out as he put his hand on the brightly colored wall.

"Wow," I replied, humbled by Russ's generosity.

"I won't be around forever. Someone else is going to have to look after her," Russ explained.

"You feel that way about all your tenants?" I asked, looking for a set of coveralls my size.

"No. She's different somehow. She's not like other people. Sometimes when she smiles..."

"...her whole face lights up," I said finishing his spoken thought.

Russ nodded quietly. I'd sort of thought the phenomenon was just from my knock on the head, but Russ had seen it too. To speak of it, neither of us was being figurative. It was as if light did shine down from her face.

I suited up throwing the strap on the box over my shoulder. My head ached vaguely, making me dizzy for a moment.

"You up for this?"

"It has been a long day, but I'll be fine, Russ. Lead on."

The big man flattened his hair back before putting on his helmet. He handed me a breathing mask as he stuck a few extra filters in his pocket. Pulling on a pair of thick gloves I stepped off the concrete platform into the slow moving water in the tunnel nearby.

Activating the illuminator on my helm did little to dispel the gloom of the underground. I was afraid of getting lost, but Russ seemed to know where he was going. After a few hundred yards the only thing that didn't change in the twisting service tunnel was a single yellow pipe. I wondered if that was what we were following, in the event we got separated somehow.

"Russ..."

"Quiet," he hissed.

"Why?" I replied, whispering.

"The Drones are fine with me wandering their territory as long as I don't make a racket."

"Drones?"

Russ shot me an angry glare, an obvious signal for me to shut up. I looked about nervously, suddenly seeing movement around every corner, and in every shadow. At the time, I knew I should have known what Drones were, but like so many other things, I couldn't remember.

All that I was able to discover so far had something to do with the outcome of placing someone who was both claustrophobic, and afflicted with amnesia, in an underground tunnel half flooded with water. It took some exerted willpower not to freak out at a couple of points where the water got high and the ceiling got low. The idea that there was some sort of creature down here with us didn't help in the slightest.

It didn't get any better, either. Russ eventually led me to a tunnel that sloped sharply downward. Clinging to a rope strung along the side, we slowly made our way deeper into the tunnels beneath Port Montaigne. The air was getting difficult to breathe, and Russ had already pulled up his breathing mask. I did the same, stepping up onto a somewhat dry concrete walkway along the side of the tunnel.

It was odd, but the more I carried the toolbox the lighter it became. The water pushed at my legs a little less and I could feel my eyes quickly becoming accustomed to the darkness. My own apprehension must have been flooding my body with adrenaline, or so I thought.

Russ paused, turning a valve adjoining the yellow pipe we'd been following then proceeded past some obvious damage to the same pipe. There was yet another valve further down that he turned, I assumed to isolate the damaged section. We returned to the damaged section and waited, breathing shallowly into our masks.

For a moment I could have sworn I heard music, or chanting, but quickly passed it off as my now very over-active imagination. Russ inspecting the damage while I waited. I couldn't tell if he was waiting for gas to clear or if he wasn't sure how to fix it. He motioned for me to set the tool box down beside him as he began fumbling with his gloves. I looked back along the edge of the tunnel, sure I heard music again.

"Russ?"

"What?"

"You hear that?"

"All I hear is you pissing your waders. Would you please shut up and hand me the flint sparker? Bit of spot welding and we can go home."

I couldn't help but smile beneath my rebreather. I wasn't an expert, but it hadn't appeared to be a two man job thus far. However, I wouldn't have wanted to come down there alone, either.

"There isn't gas down here, is there?" I asked nervously.

"Geothermal heat. It's kinda stinky but if there was that sort of buildup down here, my Canary would have gone off," Russ explained, tapping a small device attached to the front of his coveralls.

I rummaged in the tools fruitlessly for a moment until I finally located the thing he asked for. He lit up the torch and began welding a piece of metal over the gaping hole left in the pipe. I wondered what sort of folks could live in a place like this. Who were the Drones, and what made this their territory?

"Almost done."

"Russ, I'm getting a bad feeling."

"Yeah, this damage to the pipe looks like it was done on purpose."

"Really? Did it suddenly get quiet? I can't even hear the rats now," I said squinting uselessly into the blackened tunnel behind us.

Russ turned the welding torch off, lifting his heavily tinted goggles from the bridge of his nose. He scanned the tunnel looking for any movement, his ears straining for any sound. He quickly packed up the tool box and gestured for me to grab it.

"Yeah, we should go," Russ said worriedly.

"I wonder if we should have even come."

Several silhouettes appeared at the far end of the tunnel, each wearing a set of goggles that seemed to glow faintly with a strange green luminescence. Whoever they were, they seemed to be clad in loose fitting rubber wetsuits, their milky white hands clasped in front of them. They approached us peacefully with their hands raised. Their eerie and semi-translucent skin seamed to reveal every vein, muscle, and tendon in their outstretched hands.

I probably should have been more afraid than I felt. Even though they seemed non-threatening, I could see in Russ's face that he was petrified. As they drew close, one of them stepped forward removing her goggles and her rubbery cowl to reveal her face. It was pristine, and completely white like pure linen. Her large eyes were like panes of glass with fog flowing freely behind. Her mouth parted slightly to reveal almost perfect teeth as the light from our illuminators fell directly upon her.

"I'm sorry for having to damage your pipe. I really needed to talk to someone from the surface."

She spoke with a smooth voice tainted by a slight unfamiliar accent. She waited patiently for a reply. Russ and I looked at each other blankly. After a moment, I managed to find my words first, managing a weak smile.

"No harm done. What can we do for you?"

"A neighboring tribe has made several... overtures, claiming they have new allies from the surface world. They are our rivals for the scarce resources found down here."

"You need someone to either corroborate their claims, or you need some allies of your own."

"You are very perceptive, stranger."

"Silverstein."

She looked at me oddly at first, as if the sound of my name was anything but what she expected. Her large eyes seemed to look right through me, pupils dilating and constricting quickly like a camera lens. After what seemed a longer than awkward silence, she replied.

"Annabelle Five."

"You have four sisters?"

"They're clones," she said smiling slightly.

"Ah. Of course," I replied.

I'm not sure how I knew, but I was pretty sure Annabelle was joking about the clones. Her words and gestures seemed to convey more than just what one could normally perceive. All this banter was making Russ decidedly nervous. He looked over at me, eyes wide with fright. I returned a startled gaze and looked slowly behind me. I couldn't see them clearly, but there were several Drones in the water behind us, probably armed.

"Please don't be frightened. If we wanted you dead, you would be," she said, doing little to dispel our discomfort.

"I believe you. You seem very capable, so why do you need a couple of workers like us to help you?" I asked.

"He's a worker, you are something else entirely," Annabelle Five replied, looking at Russ, then over at me.

"And what am I exactly?" I asked, unsure how she knew something about me when I knew next to nothing.

"You are someone who knows the value of things," she answered.

She wasn't wrong. Numbers danced about in front of my eyes, figuratively of course, every time I got near anything resembling commerce. Every cost had a benefit to be analyzed, and my ability to pull numbers together had already become quickly apparent to me.

"There are things that can be found on the surface that can be found nowhere else. Valuable things that could give us a situational advantage down here," she explained, cocking her head to one side as if only to gaze up at me from a different perspective.

"So, you need a purchaser? Someone to represent you on the surface?"

"After a fashion, Silverstein, if that really is your name," she replied, gazing at me eerily.

"It's the only one I've got currently," I replied, trying to sound as earnest as possible.

Annabelle Five nodded while at least feigning what was pretty believable empathy for my situation. She was like the most agreeable and terrifying hostess, equal parts alluring and intimidating. It seemed as though she was genuine though, and at least as far as she knew, transparent about her stake in the agreement.

"I guess I'm in, at the very least," I said, turning to look at the building superintendent. "Russ?"

Russ nodded slowly, his eyes still wide with horror.

As we walked toward the incline in the tunnel, Annabelle Five sidled up next to me. She was taller than her cohorts, and extremely thin, her wiry hands unconsciously fidgeting with the thick belt of strange probes and contrivances worn tightly around her waist.

"You worried about me returning with your merchandise?" I asked.

"Only in being bereft. If you don't do as we've agreed, we'll just cut the power and the heat from your building. Your kind do not seem to enjoy the cold or the dark as mine do."

"I see your point. What is it I've agreed to exactly?"

"The procurement of weapons mostly, but I also need something else. I want anything colorful that can persist in this environment. I want to decorate our warrens and our tunnels, make them more beautiful than those held by our rivals. It's difficult to explain to your kind why this is important."

"No, I think I get it. You don't want them to just fear you, but envy you as well?"

"It is more primal than that, but I think your explanation is sufficient to aid you in getting us what we need."

Russ stayed quiet the rest of the walk back. I was tired, dead tired, but my head didn't hurt nearly as badly as I thought it would after exerting myself. Annabelle Five walked along beside, her silent guardians watching our every move. I could hear them click and glimpsed them gesturing to one another, speaking in an inaudible language.

"I assume you have a list, and the resources I'll need to procure the items in question?"

"Silverstein, don't you want to know what's in it for you?"

"I'm hoping we can be friends. Lately, I've found that having a good friend really makes a difference."

"I suppose that depends." Annabelle Five smiled broadly, her cold facade melting away slightly.

"I've got a connection for the colorful decoration. The weapons will be a little more difficult. I hope your friendship is going to be worth the trouble."

"You really have no fear of us, do you?" Annabelle Five observed. "Not the sort that comes from loathing or ignorance anyway."

I looked back at Annabelle's crew and saw no malice in them whatsoever. No hateful gazes or projected hostility. They were there just to keep each other safe and ask for help in the only way they probably could. There was no hidden agenda here, just what passed as commerce in Downtown Port Montaigne.

"You've been very polite, and your caution is definitely warranted where 'my kind' are concerned," I replied.

"Most humans I've spoken to are arrogant, believing you're our betters merely for being what created us. You don't carry the same attitude," Annabelle observed, probing somewhat as we walked back through the higher water.

"I guess I didn't know, but might have assumed that was the case," I replied, marveling at how she could carry on a conversation in a dark tunnel with water almost up to your shoulders.

"You are very mysterious, Silverstein," and that was all she said the rest of the way back until we reached the landing that led to Taylor's building.

"You still have a good feeling about this?" I asked, looking to Annabelle.

Annabelle Five smiled wryly, handing me a knapsack made of the rubber inner-tube one finds in a tire, the strap crafted of an old lap belt. I gazed inside at the contents, nodding to Annabelle Five.

"If you do this for me, you will have my trust, and I'll try to be that good friend you're looking for."

I nodded stepping up into Russ's prep area. When I turned back to wave goodbye, Annabelle Five and her friends were gone. I could only smile weakly at Russ, sensing his apprehension relative to the whole affair.

"This is on you, Silverstein. I'll have no part of it." Russ stated quietly.

"No problem. You've got a building full of tenants to take care of."

Russ paused, considering his next words carefully.

"You're welcome to stay in for the time being," he said a little quieter.

"Thanks. Let me know if you need any more help."

Russ just grunted as he hung up his waders.

"You ever actually seen Drones before? That was what those were right?" I asked.

"I knew they were there, but I'd never actually seen one until today. I hope I never see one again," Russ replied.

He looked as though he needed a stiff drink, and I wasn't too far from being in the same state. We made our way up the steel ladder, and after handing Russ his tool box he gave me a hand up. I was glad to be back on the surface and did not relish the idea of going back into the tunnels.

I knew I needed to follow through. The Drones would be very valuable allies if I needed to cut and run. I knew Taylor would be good for helping me find things to decorate an underground labyrinth of tunnels occupied by those strange creatures, but finding weapons was something else entirely. I hoped I could make good on my promise.

The elevator was down, so I took the stairs to Taylor's floor and knocked on her door. She appeared a second later, pinching her nose at the sight of me. I laughed playfully shoving past her and made a mad dash for the bathroom. I breathed a heavy sigh of relief as I vigorously washed my hands.

"Everything go okay?"

"I met the Drones."

"You mean the scary tunnel people that steal people in their sleep, drown them, and eat them?"

"Yeah, them."

"Well, at least the heat's back on."

"They want me to do them a favor."

"Who?"

"The Drones."

"Oh, of course they do."

I laid out the contents of the rubber tire knapsack to dispel Taylor's incredulity. She gazed at the pile of money and the very short list with intense interest. She smiled looking at the list.

"They want an interior decorator?"

"And weapons."

"I am sure I can help you with one, but you might need to talk to Joe about the other."

"What's Joe into?"

"Sometimes the people he pays for protection ask him to store things."

"What kinds of things?"

"All kinds of things."

I gathered up the Drone's money and list into the knapsack. Taylor just sat looking bemused for a moment, sliding off her well-worn couch to the floor. She wandered over to the wall and popped open a tub of paint and began rendering some ideas for decorations suitable for a wet tunnel environment.

"Aren't you going to ask me what's in it for you?"

"I assumed you were asking for my help as a friend."

"I guess I was. Thank you."

CHAPTER 4

Downtown, Port Montaigne – Strip n' Waffle

10:51 PM, December 21st, 2199

Silverstein's Log, Part 3

I sat outside the Strip and Waffle on an old bus bench, wondering how I was going to ask Joe to set up a gun buy for me. I didn't even know if the guy had those kinds of connections. He might even be insulted I asked him such a thing. I was probably way out of my league, punching above my weight class, etcetera.

I'd just about made up my mind to go in and talk to Joe when a well-dressed and exceedingly elderly man sat down next to me. He was dressed in a dark green suit, burgundy tie, and matching hat. He turned and looked at me, almost as if he expected me to say hello. He was damnably familiar, the only person I'd met since losing my memory that evoked that sensation.

He furrowed his brow, looking into my face, like he wasn't sure of what he was seeing. Then, he smiled, tipped his hat to me and pulled out a cigarette. It was not the hand rolled type that Taylor and the rest of downtown smoked.

The smell was intoxicating. In what was my very short memory, I couldn't recall ever wanting a cigarette. All the same, I wanted one of his cigarettes. I looked over at him and searched for the words.

"I'm surprised you don't have any of your own," he said, offering me one.

"Not sure why you would think that."

He smiled and pulled out a stainless steel lighter and lit the cigarette, puffed once, and handed it to me. The cigarette tasted as good as it smelled. I even seemed to breathe easier as the smoke filled my lungs. The sensation was fantastic.

"That's the good stuff my friend. Pure tobacco grown in the black earth," the gentleman replied.

"You and I sitting here isn't some strange coincidence, is it?" I asked, continuing to enjoy the cigarette.

"No."

"Who are you?"

"You really don't know? I'd feared as much, but I guess it doesn't really matter at this point. I only have another three minutes or so to live."

"Not a lot of time to get to know each other."

The gentleman took out a wooden box and placed the stainless steel lighter inside of it with two dozen of those wonderful cigarettes. He handed me the box and smiled. I couldn't help but be completely baffled by the situation, so I stared down at the box and listened. "It's peculiar, talking with you like this. A stone bench on a corner in downtown Port Montaigne, chatting like we're old friends."

I nodded slightly, possessing not a single clue what he was talking about.

"You look good. Well, better than most of the rest of us. I don't know how you managed to beat it. How did you achieve even a measure of control?"

"I don't know what you're talking about," I replied, shaking my head.

"Really? Maybe you aren't one of us. Maybe you're... him? That makes sense, especially after I saw your eyes light up when I lit up. You always did like the good stuff."

"I do like them. Try and take them from me," I replied with a wink.

"You don't know who you are?" The old man said slowly clasping his hands together.

"No."

"Hell of a thing. How'd it happen?"

I lifted up my hair and showed the old codger my stitches. He winced and shook his head.

"You do that to yourself? I suppose, directly, or indirectly, you probably did."

"Not sure."

"Well don't expect me to ruin it for you. Also, I doubt it was a blow to the head that has suppressed your memory."

"Ruin what? What else could it have been?"

"I think if you had even the slightest inkling of who you were, you'd probably thank me for not telling you. At least, right this moment anyway," the old man said leaning back slightly.

"Maybe you should let me be the judge of that?"

I looked over at him, hopeful for any illumination into who I was, but he was gone. It was strange, but I was suddenly possessed of a profound sadness, more than what I thought was usual. Some part of me knew this old man, and the rest wondered why he had come to visit me so close to what he knew would be his death.

Of all the things in the world one would choose to do with their last moments, why would they visit me? I reached over and closed his eyes. I went ahead and checked his pockets, but didn't have any identification on him, just the cigarettes and the lighter. I stood up and looked at the old guy for a couple of moments. There was definitely something familiar about him, but like so much of everything else, I couldn't place him. I inspected his hands carefully. There were no callouses or scars suggesting he'd led anything but the life of an uptown person.

Joe came out of the Strip and Waffle and lit up one of his hand-rolled monstrosities. He looked over at me, then the old man, with eyebrows raised, and cigarette hanging at an odd angle from his mouth. Putting his hands in his pockets he wandered over to me.

"Who's the old guy?"

"Didn't get a chance to find out. He knew who I was though."

"Wow, really? Y'know, he does look a little bit like you. A relative maybe?"

"Yeah, maybe. Joe, I need to ask you something."

"Shoot."

"Well, I've got a client that needs some special items."

"Uh-huh."

"I don't want to get Taylor in trouble, but she said maybe you could help me?"

Joe's face broke into a barely contained smile.

"She's already talked to you," I said covering my face with my hands.

"You're a nice guy, Silverstein. She knew it would take you an hour to build up the nerve."

I nodded, resigned to the fact that I probably wasn't cut out for the type of business regularly conducted downtown. Joe patted me on the shoulder reassuringly, while finishing his cigarette. I gave the old guy a last look before we went inside. He seemed peaceful, and not eerily so.

"I'll have a couple of guys deal with the body," Joe said, beckoning for me to follow him.

We walked into the kitchen toward the back where the industrial freezers stood. He was either going to kill me, show me the merchandise I was after, or give me an ice cream and send me home. Turns out, the freezer marked 'out of order' housed a number of crates.

Joe opened one revealing a number of matte black firearms resting in yellowing wax paper. He tipped one up out of the crate holding it by its not-so-shiny barrel for me to inspect. One gun looked pretty much the same as the other to me.

"I have no idea what I'm looking at," I admitted softly, shaking my head.

"These are expensive and foreign made. Very good guns, but difficult to get ammunition for," Joe remarked. He gently closed the crate.

He opened another crate that held several grey colored firearms, smaller with shrouds I guessed were painted up to be urban camouflage. Joe grabbed one up and put it in my hands. It was unbelievably light and the clip which fed the ammunition was made of a clear polycarbonate or similar.

"These are pretty common around here, and additive manufactured. No one gang or organization is known specifically for using them, and the ammunition is easy to get. These are cheaper, though, and can jam up if not maintained properly."

I nodded quietly as I awkwardly looked the firearm over. Joe opened the last and smallest crate and withdrew a semi-gloss revolver with a dark wooden handle. He clicked the cylinder open. It carried seven rounds of ammunition.

"These are good backup pieces in a pinch," Joe said raising his shirt to show that he carried one wedged into his belt. "Very accurate, and very reliable."

"Who makes and manufactures these weapons?" I asked, looking through the revolvers.

"Armor Company makes the carbines I showed you," Joe said as he pointed to the matte black rifles.

I nodded somberly in response.

"Texlar Industries makes the grey submachine guns, and Smith & Wesson makes these revolvers."

If I had ever heard of any of those manufacturers I couldn't remember. My curiosity sated, I began gathering a selection of each, grabbing two of the carbines, a half dozen submachine guns, and a dozen revolvers. I packed as much ammunition as I could afford into black duffle bags Joe was kind enough to provide me.

"Taylor didn't tell me who you were doing the buy for. Do I want to know?"

"Nope."

I took a quick look at Joe's books while I was there then waited with a plate of waffles while Taylor finished her shift. She bounded into Joe's office just before quitting time, nearly tripping over the black duffle bags. A little red in the face, she stooped down to look through what I'd bought from Joe.

"Jeez, did you leave any money for me to buy decorations?" she asked, pointing a revolver at me.

"Yes! Yes!" I exclaimed, holding my hands in the air.

We sat in the back room and chatted quietly with a couple of the dancers until it was almost dawn. We didn't want to walk through downtown in the dead of night with duffle bags full of weapons. Borrowing one of Joe's laundry carts, we covered them with old curtains and set out for home.

The sun's rays barely made it down through the raised uptown streets during any time that wasn't dawn or dusk. Even though I had no idea how to use one, I loaded and tucked one of the revolvers into my belt in case we ran into trouble. As the few visible uptown lights began to fade, the street got busy.

The abandoned buildings seemed to disgorge people of every type and persuasion. Scavengers, day laborers, dock workers, and more flooded the streets around us. The laundry cart was a cunning camouflage. A bag lady offered to buy the curtains, but that was the closest we came to our cover being blown.

Taylor did as she always did, weaving expertly through the crowd giving pick pockets the shove, while I played mule. A decent arrangement considering I couldn't tell a hustler from a missionary down here. Everyone seemed to blend together, only the value of what they carried, and their relative earning potential seemed to rise to the top. As usual, all I could see were the numbers.

I still couldn't remember a single detail about myself, but I could tell each one of these street walkers the best way to invest the money they panhandled. I could advise them on the best way to write off business expenses, balance their checkbooks, and plan for the college their kids will probably never attend. This sometimes-useful ability had become more and more troubling.

It wasn't that I was ungrateful for having a skill in the wake of losing my memory, but seeing people as just numbers had begun to wear thin. The only person that my overly mechanical mind couldn't seem to quantify were the drones and Taylor. With them it wasn't about numbers or money, it was something else.

The building where Taylor lived was a welcome sight. It was some considerable trouble getting the laundry cart up the crumbling front stairs. Between the two of us, we managed to make it into the lobby before the rain started. Russ greeted us with a stern face, and angry eyes that moved slowly down to our muddy feet.

"Sorry!" Taylor squeaked, quickly retreating to the threshold to kick off her shoes.

He just shook his head and resumed mopping the lobby floor. Russ looked over at me, his eyes darting toward the cart suggestively. I nodded an affirmative to him. He resumed his mopping while looking back out into the street nervously.

He was right to be nervous. We were insane for having done this at all, but this had become about more than just keeping the heat and power on in the building. Yes, I wanted to help Taylor, but I also had come to believe that I hadn't been merely discarded in downtown Port Montaigne. The old man's appearance and the things he said threw any notion of my situation being accidental into question.

If getting the laundry cart into the barely functioning elevator wasn't bad enough, there wasn't room for the cart in Taylor's apartment. I had little choice, so we stashed it on the roof after unloading the weapons. Needless to say, my limbs ached and my head throbbed mercilessly by the time we got to the apartment and shut the door. Nevertheless, I spent another twenty minutes preparing some ramen to eat before we crashed.

"One of the girls told me you found a dead guy outside the club."

"Yeah, he gave me these before he died," I said pulling the slim wooden box of cigarettes from my coat pocket.

Taylor opened the box withdrawing the lighter and a cigarette. Her nose wrinkled at the smell of the contents and quickly closed the box handing it back to me. I smiled quietly and replaced it back in my pocket between stirring the ramen.

"What are those awful things?"

"It's real tobacco. It wasn't grown in a greenhouse or in a flower box off someone's window downtown like those things you prefer to smoke... and no, you can't have any of mine."

"If you're going to insult my smokes, don't bother trying to bum one from me when you run out of your fancy cigars," she replied, her voice full of mirth.

"Have I ever asked you for one?"

"No, in fact I didn't think you smoked."

"Never wanted one until the old guy smoked one of these in front of me. They must have been my brand before I got conked on the head."

"Only uptown folks can afford those things. You never see them down here."

"Yeah, that occurred to me too. That old boy was dressed like uptown, sort of like when you found me. Even had a pair of Silverstein shoes. He knew who I was, but told me I'd probably prefer not to know."

"Really?"

"I told him I'd prefer to judge that for myself, but he died before he could tell me any more."

"That's really strange, and a little scary, Silverstein. You didn't happen to um... take his shoes?"

"Taylor, the only thing I took was what he gave me. I haven't gotten to the really odd part, though. The old guy knew, down to the minute, how much time he had left to live."

Taylor was silent for a few moments, watching as I added a blend of frozen peas and carrots to the ramen. I gave the concoction another minute before pulling it off the stove to her makeshift strainer. The steam from the boiling water rose and fogged up the few windows in the apartment.

"This is pretty good. Did you suddenly remember how to cook?" Taylor joked as she greedily devoured my creation.

"Nope," I replied holding up the printed directions on the back of the package.

Taylor laughed, another of a precious few genuine displays of glee I'd witnessed since we met. She helped me finish mine before crashing on her bed in the adjoining room. I moved to my own spot on the couch and closed my eyes hoping the blessed sleep would take me quickly.

The rain continued to make its way down through the tangle of concrete that held uptown Port Montaigne above. There was a palpable sense of déjà vu that overcame me just as I drifted off to sleep, like my mind was desperately grasping to recall what came before whatever happened to me in the alley. Our brains probably need more than just the little I had to give the body motion. I fell asleep contemplating the notion.

I was nudged awake hours later by an impossibly thin Drone, his green luminescent goggles the only light in the apartment. He shushed me, his pointy ears straining to pick up even the smallest sound. I grabbed the revolver from my belt and held it up clumsily.

"Are you the man called Silverstein?" the Drone hissed as he flicked the pistol from my hand. Then, he perched on my chest and stared down at me.

I nodded, quickly gasping for breath. The Drone looked about the apartment, his eyes settling on the duffle bags. I grabbed him by his rubbery trench coat and we rolled roughly to the carpet. He gave me two quick punches to the solar plexus knocking the wind from me, then tossed me against the couch.

The Drone's semi-translucent skin seemed to glow with the dim green light of his goggles, reflecting off the rest of his garments. He was still wet from the rain falling quietly outside, but there was no breeze in the apartment suggesting an open window. I couldn't fathom how he'd gotten in, as all twenty of Taylor's locks were still firmly in place.

The slender Drone seemed more than hyper-vigilant, almost paranoid for a few moments. Then he calmed, moving toward the small window in Taylor's living room. His hands were powerful, each ending in wicked retractable claws. He was barely over five feet in height belying his monstrous strength.

He looked back over to where I gasped for breath, and after removing his goggles, turned to keep a sort of watch out the window. I staggered over to where he was standing and gestured toward the kitchen.

"Coffee? Tea? Or are you just going to wander about looking creepy and beating the stuffing out of me?"

"My name is Ezra One. Annabelle Five sent me to check on you. We got word that our rivals down below, a group calling themselves the Sodality, have gotten wind of your movements."

"How do I know you are not part of the Sodality?" I replied, still gasping for air.

"I'd have killed you in your sleep and taken the guns, and the girl."

"Fair enough. If they're the Sodality, what do you guys call yourselves?"

"We don't call ourselves anything. We used to be part of the Underground Republic. Since the leadership split apart, it has been chaos."

I stood and recovered my revolver. Keeping Ezra in sight, I turned and looked in on Taylor who was sleeping like a stone. I looked quickly back at Ezra who was suddenly standing uncomfortably close to me.

"Silverstein, we should move the guns," he remarked quietly, his paranoia almost contagious.

"Your enemies might be counting on us to do that. I thought you guys didn't operate above ground."

Ezra One hesitated, looking self-conscious for a moment. I marveled at how every emotion Ezra seemed to feel was clearly rendered on his face. Even in my short interactions with Drones, they all seemed emotionally distant. Distant seemed an inadequate description however. Impervious, perhaps?

"Often, it is not a matter of willingness, but ability," Ezra hissed. "The way many of us were engineered it grants an almost paralyzing fear of wide open spaces. That won't stop our rivals from sending their above ground allies to intercept these weapons." He pressed his ear to the front door.

"You're operating above ground," I replied coolly.

"We need to move the weapons, and the sooner the better," he replied narrowing his eyes to my question.

"Why can't we just descend through the access beneath this building and make the delivery?" I asked, not fully understanding his presence.

"That way has been compromised and is no longer safe."

Drones from the rival tribe were waiting for us down there. How could they have learned of what we intended to do so quickly? The sinking feeling in the pit of my stomach grew two sizes.

Taylor stepped out of her room and shuffled past me toward the bathroom. She'd almost made it before letting out a shrill scream as she caught sight of Ezra. She grabbed a pair of shears from her sewing basket and brandished them in his direction menacingly. It took me several moments to calm her, almost forgetting she's never seen a Drone before.

"Taylor, this is Ezra One. Ezra, Taylor," I stammered, wrapping my arms around Taylor.

"He's gross! Are these the things that we're getting the guns and decorations for?!" she blurted angrily, swinging the shears about in random, dangerous arcs.

Ezra put on an uneasy smile allowing his claws to retract back into his slender hands. "Your hair is very pretty, and we will be indeed fortunate if the decorations you provide us are half as colorful," Ezra said quickly, backing away submissively.

Taylor's demeanor instantly changed to one of the friendly host. Without missing a beat she began showing Ezra a fan of color samples. The small Drone warmed to her quickly and looked on with genuine interest at what she had to offer. I let the two of them get acquainted while I put the coffee on. It wasn't going to be easy to move the guns discretely.

As seemed to be the case with everyone, once Taylor turned on the charm, there wasn't anyone she couldn't win over. She even gave Ezra a knitted skullcap she'd made for herself when she was younger. It fit him perfectly, the rainbow pattern standing in stark contrast to the rest of his sinister appearance. It took every iota of willpower I possessed not to laugh at the peculiar sight. However, Ezra was completely moved by the gift. It was clear as day on his eerily smooth face. It was as though no one had ever given him anything before. He took the small hat off and gazed at it lovingly before tucking it safely away.

It did strike me as very strange how we all became such fast friends, or at least acquaintances. Ezra only got calmer the more interaction he had with us, and Taylor talked to him with an ease that she seemed to only have with me. Ezra was like us in a way I surmised, not like the others of his kind, outcast, and unique by choice or circumstance.

"Ezra, besides this building, do you know of any way down to the part of the tunnels your people control?" I asked as I handed Taylor a cup of coffee.

"The nearest way down, isn't very close. The Alderman Company concrete factory," Ezra replied.

"We could stash the guns, and Ezra, in the laundry cart and hoof it?" Taylor smirked.

I couldn't tell if Ezra was more concerned with the coffee I'd offered him, or the prospect of pretending to be dirty laundry for several hours. Regardless, we all eventually agreed that it would be best to make for the concrete factory. Ezra had to be bribed with a handful of colorful rubber bracelets plucked from Taylor's arm to be coaxed into the laundry cart.

It was an arduous journey pushing the cart from one district of downtown to another. The cart served well enough, but adding Ezra to the cart only made it more difficult to navigate the broken streets and haphazard alleys. Taylor picked a good route, or at least one that was fairly direct and lacking a lot of other foot traffic. I observed how much of downtown was dark all the time, devoid of light or people, and wondered how such had come to pass.

It was as though there had been great plans for the city, a means to rejuvenate every row, home, and shop. Then, something terrible happened and rather than take the time to continue with the original plan, the city built over the top of the blemish. Port Montaigne was not without dignity, but it had an equal measure of shame to go with it.

Our destination, nestled within the industrial district, was utterly dark sitting on a rise just below the bowels of uptown. Even when compared to the rest of downtown, this place was dark lacking any ambient light from the surrounding areas. The sky was blotted out by overpasses and the underbellies of huge buildings. Waste water and soot rained down upon us there as we pushed toward the loading area beside a massive concrete factory.

The touch screen on Taylor's mobile and a small flashlight Ezra had with him were our only light sources. As we stopped to rest, I gazed over at what little I could see of the front gate. There were fresh tracks in the ground left by wheeled vehicles, the newly broken hinges of the gate still shiny not having had time to properly corrode. Someone was already inside lying in wait, and we were probably out of options.

"Should we go back?" she whispered, looking under the curtains at Ezra.

"Risky either way," Ezra replied, shaking his head.

"There's a silt pit along the side that's fallen in leaving a gap below that wall," Taylor said pointing.

It took all of us to lift the cart in through the wall, and over the fallen rubble. We were as quiet as possible as we crept past the large heaps of abandoned gravel. The place was eerily quiet, not even the cooing of pigeons or squeaking of bats could be heard overhead.

Loose gravel crunched beneath our feet as the cart wheels squeaked faintly. In spite of our best attempts to be quiet, we weren't very stealthy. I could only hope whoever else was in the cement plant was too busy or far away to hear us. Really, I just hoped we'd get lucky.

I was already nervous, which quickly began to turn into a bad feeling about the whole affair. My fears were realized as we stepped into the lower loading area, almost to the drainage access we sought. Suddenly, the lights of three vehicles blinked on, bright light spilling into the area. Several figures exited the vehicles and approached us, guns drawn.

I had never seen any of them before, and Taylor was the first to raise her hands. My mind raced as I glanced about for any means of escape. There was none.

"Kind of you to bring us the package, really saved us a lot of trouble" one of them remarked, pressing the barrel of his gun painfully against my cheek. "The girl is a nice bonus."

He lifted me up by my shirt, relieving me of my weapon, then lifted the curtains on the cart. I took a sharp breath as he did, noticing that Ezra was conspicuously missing. The exertion and stress of the situation took its toll as my head began to ache once more.

Suddenly the lights on one of the vehicles went dark, then another, and another, blanketing the area in blessed darkness. I dropped to the ground and began crawling for Taylor, who stood frozen in place. Then there were screams, and muzzle flashes as the goons began firing at shadows. I grabbed Taylor and threw her to the ground, rolling over on top of her.

I glanced up, seeing only flashes of what was going on in time with the muzzle flare. Ezra was leaping between them lithely clawing out eyes, taking hands off at the wrists, and opening up throats with deadly precision. He landed on one man's chest clawing him, and then leapt to another, his serrated hands raking something vital in each one. For a moment, the numbers vanished. I was afraid. I looked away, holding Taylor down under me as bullets flew about randomly.

Then, as quickly as the chaos begun, the screams and gunfire abated. The sound of someone's labored breathing ceased with a sickening gurgle. The headlights on one of the vehicles flicked back on, revealing a charnel house around us, blood oozing across the ground toward where Taylor and I lay. Ezra withdrew his clawed hand from the interior of car, and walked over to where Taylor and I sat terrified.

"You guys alright?" Ezra asked quietly as he wiped his clawed hands on the shirt of a fallen goon.

"Where did you learn to fight like that?" she questioned after a long pause.

Ezra didn't respond. Instead, he deftly fished a wallet out of the pocket of one of the fallen goons. He gazed inside, then dropped it, kicking it over to me. I took a gander inside the wallet then let it drop back to the ground. According to the ID, they were members of a Martian paramilitary group called Nomad Incorporated. I'd never heard of them, but it did mean something.

"Who hires this kind of muscle, from another planet, to intercept a few thousand worth of weapons?" Taylor asked. She shook her head after fishing through the wallet for spare change.

"I don't think they were here after the guns. One of these guns is worth more than our entire haul, and all the ammunition they are using is custom," Ezra said, gazing down at the goon's expensive looking hardware.

I walked back over to the laundry cart and set about opening every crate. In one marked as ammunition for the revolvers there were several stainless steel vials. They were unmarked but stamped with the usual industrial warning labels identifying them as containing a hazardous substance. I looked over at Ezra who seemed as genuinely surprised as I was.

"We got set up," I remarked closing the crate back up.

"Who knew we would be coming here?" Taylor asked nervously.

"Someone who knew where you live, knew we had the goods, and could listen in on our plans," I replied quietly.

"Russ or Joe? They are the only ones that could have known," she replied, her voice quivering with worry.

"In either case, the room would have had to be bugged."

"There is another possibility," Ezra interrupted our paranoia-fest.

Both Taylor and I looked over at Ezra who seemed more grim than usual.

"There are Drones with clairvoyant abilities. However, in every case, such a Drone has been an Elder, garnering their powers later in life," he remarked coldly.

"I thought you said the leadership had disbanded, like not around anymore, right?"

Ezra turned toward me pushing his goggles up to the top of his head. I could see he was worried, his smooth face creased with anxiety. I did my best to throw salve on his fears.

"Hey, we don't know anything for sure. Maybe Russ or Joe betrayed us, bugged Taylor's apartment, and used us as unwitting mules to transport an unknown chemical agent?"

"What if the Sodality has captured an Elder and are forcing them to use their second sight to quietly manipulate the surface world? We could have a big problem," he remarked sadly.

"Should we take their guns and add them to what we already have?" Taylor asked. She tried to avoid looking down at the slaughter that lay all around us.

"No. We'd need special caseless ammunition," Ezra remarked giving one of the guns a gentle, dismissive kick.

He handed me the crate with the chemical agent and pushed the rest down a drainage hole nearby. He waved us a quick goodbye and promised to meet up with us in a couple of days to get the decorations. On the way out I recovered my revolver and the ID cards carried by one of the mercenaries. I tucked the box of chemical agent under one arm and grasped Taylor's hand with the other.

"Silverstein, do you think Russ or Joe sold us out?"

"Do you?"

"I don't know. When the alternative is psychic mutants watching you from the underground? I almost hope one of them did. We'll look for bugs when we get back to the apartment."

"You think it is safe to go back there?"

"You think the elderly underground mutants can't watch you showering somewhere else?"

"I'm serious!" Taylor yelled and slugged me playfully. "We could be in real trouble here!"

I paused to look down at her. Her lips trembled as she broke gaze with me. I'd just made her life endlessly more complex and I was beginning to feel more than a little guilty about it.

I couldn't shake the feeling that all of this was somehow connected to the life I led before waking in the alley. Somehow, I was playing a game where I was only allowed the briefest glimpse at the pieces. I didn't know how to fix this.

"I'm sorry, Taylor. I thought this would be a simple thing. Get the Drones what they want, keep the heat on in your building, and everyone wins."

"We could run. You might never find out who you are, but at least we'd be safe."

"I don't know. After talking to that old guy before, I get the feeling I'm in this predicament because I ran from my problems in the first place."

"You sound like the narrator in one of those after-school specials."

"They still do those?"

"No, it's just something people say I guess. Let's go."

We crept out of the cement factory and out into the open industrial park. We made our way across the open ground to the darkened buildings and warehouses at the fringe of the populated part of downtown. It was a long walk home, but blissfully uneventful.

"What do you think of Ezra?" Taylor said breaking the silence.

"I'm really not sure. He seems very genuine though, almost like he was incapable of lying."

"Corporations created the Drones to work in the underground places humans were unwilling to go," Taylor said gazing at some text on her mobile. "Is it possible that one of those corporations made Drones designed to be weapons?"

"Entirely possible, but why would they make them so small? Ezra can't be more than seventy-five pounds."

I stashed the crate containing the mystery chemical agent beneath a bit of concrete behind Taylor's building. Once I was certain no one was watching, we crept inside through the back entrance, and set about searching her apartment. We had no idea what we were looking for but found nothing resembling a bug.

The thing that didn't figure into all this was that they knew we were going to the concrete factory, but not that Ezra was with us. The goons had no idea he would be there, but seemed to be expecting Taylor and I. That would point to Joe or Russ, except that we couldn't find any surveillance equipment in Taylor's apartment. It was a puzzle.

"Taylor, where is it?"

"Maybe they came in and removed the bug while we were gone? I don't know."

"We aren't exactly master spies or detectives. It could still be here in the apartment, and we're too blind to see it."

"This sucks," Taylor said plopping down on the couch.

"I agree. Let's pack a bag and get out of here."

CHAPTER 5

Downtown, Port Montaigne - Porter's District

5:20 AM, May 15th, 2178 - 21 years previous to shutdown.

Perfidy looked down at the wreckage that remained of the transport spread across the street, then up at the hole in the uptown substructure above. It had plummeted from at least ten thousand feet and crashed down through a quarter mile worth of all that separated uptown from downtown. Natural gas burned as sewage and clean water alike trickled down from the damage above.

There were emergency crews and city engineers just arriving and they were already counting bodies. Perfidy could see none small enough to be what he was sent here to confirm. The Cabal had potentially lost an important asset as a result of the accident, if it could really be classified as such, and it was up to him to find it.

Those that dwelled in Downtown Port Montaigne had already spent the last thirty minutes following the crash, grabbing up anything they could recycle or sell. The scene was heavily compromised and if the asset had been lying about, it was long gone now. As impossible as it seemed, he was probably going to seek out anyone that trafficked in human beings for what he sought.

Perfidy looked about the area with his mechanical eyes until he spotted someone carrying more biological matter than was normal for a person his size. The man had a neoprene sack full of body parts he'd gathered from the wreck and was heading off quickly to avoid the impending arrival of law enforcement. Perfidy followed him for several blocks, the clamor of the crash scene fading slowly behind him.

The man's heat signature was easy to spot in the crowd as the body parts he carried slowly cooled and began to release a myriad of gases easy to trace by someone with mechanically and chemically enhanced senses. The man stopped at an ice house, a place set aside to use the chemical exchange that fueled the air conditioners that kept uptown comfortable as a contrived means to generate and sell ice. Illegal, but far from the focus of law enforcement when they dared to venture downtown for any reason.

Perfidy let himself in, the man's visual and chemical signature guiding him from the street through several cold rooms to a back room where he detected several men and one woman. The room was cold, and lined with wooden slats and commercial thickness cardboard for insulation. There were several cribs heated with convection style space heaters and cupboards of formula and baby food.

The men and woman looked up at Perfidy in surprise as he entered the room. One went for a handgun, but Perfidy already had his own in hand, leveled at the man's face. All were dressed as one might expect someone living downtown, like discarded hand-me-downs. The woman had a lab coat on, and wore a clean pair of gloves.

"I'm looking for a child, about two years old, female," Perfidy said, turning his obviously mechanical eyes toward the woman.

"We have several, and they can be altered to suit. I assume you're here shopping for someone else?" the woman responded nervously.

"No, I'm looking for a specific child. She'd have come in very recently, within the last hour," Perfidy replied coolly, handgun held on the guard.

"We don't buy them that way, we've a farm and--"

"Who does?" Perfidy interrupted the woman.

"Devils," she replied.

"Excuse me?" Perfidy replied, comically pretending as if he hadn't heard her.

"That's what they call themselves, or Red Coats some people call them. They don't have a lab or a farm so they buy and sell," the woman replied.

Perfidy knew leaving any of them alive was against procedure, but he would have to shoot the infants as well. He wondered if he even had a soul to fetter with such actions, but he wasn't going to shoot the kids or leave them without minders to freeze to death either. He shot the guard in the face, turning his gun quickly toward the woman. She gave out a short scream as Perfidy grabbed her and watched the others scramble away for their lives.

"I'll know if you told anyone I was here. I'll come back, and I'll do worse than kill you. Do you know what a Skin Slave is?" Perfidy said, his tone even and professional.

"Y-yes, I know what one is," the woman said shaking in terror.

Perfidy let her go and went over to one of the cribs. The infant was startled by the loud noise, but was the only one that hadn't started crying. The child reached up grasping at the air as Perfidy holstered his sidearm.

"This is when we learn to want," Perfidy whispered, pulling a small blanket up over the child, his mechanical eyes sensing its body temperature was lower than what would have been comfortable.

He stepped out of the cold house knowing one of the men who fled would likely approach a Red Coat to tell of a man with mechanical eyes. He decided to follow the signature of the thinnest of the group, and likely the hungriest. He was heading east toward the under-harbor, a good sign. The other downtown dwellers parted as they pushed past him going about their business.

Perfidy knew he was an oddity down here, but the time for subtlety had ended. It had been almost three hours since the crash and the window of opportunity for reacquiring the asset was beginning to close. He followed the hungry man relentlessly, scoffing quietly at some of the precautions he took to avoid being followed. Apparently, he had some understanding of his capabilities, which meant there were likely cyborgs among the Red Coats.

The under-harbor was mostly owned by oil companies that employed welders and ship-builders to make repairs to their huge and rapidly aging fleet of tankers. Some of the tankers were the size of military aircraft carriers and there were only a handful of harbors deep enough to accommodate them. Silt draggers and other countermeasures work around the clock to keep the Port Montaigne harbor ideal and the money flowing upward.

Perfidy hadn't been down here for years, but little had changed in that time. Soot covered, and ramshackle living accommodations clung to the support structure beneath the primary harbor some forty feet overhead, echoing with the sounds of heavy equipment further east near the water. It was dark, and Perfidy was relying on his own enhanced senses to travel away from the more common means of ingress to the interior of the under-harbor.

Dock workers walked back and forth, going to and from work not far away as Perfidy followed his quarry along the final legs to what was a forbidding and decidedly secret location. The entrance had been constructed between two long abandoned pipelines that hadn't been used to transport oil in probably fifty years. Reaching them required a special knowledge of the area and all its many underground passages and portals. Perfidy hoped he'd be able to remember the way out once he'd finished.

The entrance was unguarded and unlocked. They were either very careless, or they already knew they had a visitor. There was no choice at this point but to head in and deal with whatever lay in wait. The interior hall was constructed and reformed pipe, bent to a roughly oblong shape and allowing access by a single person at a time to the interior.

The first chamber was large, almost thirty feet in diameter, and set up to be guarded from several fortified positions made of metal sheets welded together in a semi-circle at both far corners. The floor was made of salvaged expanded metal that met with walls made of metal sheeting riveted together across an unseen frame.

No one guarded the room but a single older gentleman smoking a cigarette. The tobacco was imported and the man stank of chemicals common to longevity treatments. Both odors oozed from the man's pores, if Perfidy's enhanced senses were to be trusted.

"Hello. I assume you aren't here to buy or sell?" the elderly man asked, sticking to the shadows in the doorframe.

"No."

"Your senses won't work as effectively in here as you'd like. We've taken measures to avoid the attention of law enforcement and customs agents."

"I'm here to find an infant, likely recovered from the wreckage of a transport that fell through Uptown, the substructure beneath, and the Downtown streets below," Perfidy stated patiently.

"That crash happened scarcely a few hours ago," the elder man said as he smoked. "What makes you think she was brought here?"

"If you know about the crash, you probably know why," Perfidy replied.

"She'd have to be pretty special to have survived, or the equipment used to transport her was anyway."

"Something like that," Perfidy replied, betraying no emotion.

"If she gets bought or sold, I'll let you know," the old man replied. "If I can procure her, is there a finder's fee?"

"I'm not authorized to make any deals," Perfidy replied.

"I don't have to let you leave this place," the elderly man said, crushing out what remained of his cigarette on the door frame.

Perfidy stood, waiting for the other shoe to drop. The old man stepped into room, the light illuminating his varied features. Perfidy could see a man ravaged by addiction to surgical procedure, his features having been altered too many times probably to count. He wore a red jacket adorned with a single set of demonic horns that curled back from his chest to the collarbones.

"I'll look for the girl, if she's to be found. I'll procure her, and you'll pay me to hand her over," the old man offered, looking back at the darkened fortified positions.

"I never said I was looking for a girl," Perfidy replied, drawing his sidearm in one fluid motion.

The room filled with gunfire as the old man lunged forward and several cloaked cyborgs opened fire. Perfidy threw himself to the floor and rolled backward. It wasn't quick enough, and the old man was on him now, foot falls from unseen guards coming up quickly behind him. The metal structure echoed oddly, playing havoc with Perfidy's senses as he struggled with the inhumanly strong trafficker.

The old man clawed savagely at Perfidy, his fingernails altered to be as hard as steel. Sparks flew as Perfidy rolled clear and bolted for the door. Rounds fired from guns loaded with caseless ammunition punched through the steel wall and floor around him as his auditory dampeners activated. The dark exterior of the building welcomed Perfidy as he moved quickly out of the path of continuing small arms fire.

"Confirmed contact," Perfidy said, activating an auditory implant.

The signal didn't go far down here, and he knew it was unlikely his handler would hear the transmission. He tried again anyway. No response.

He knelt down beside the entrance and waited for pursuit, but there was none. The whole area went suddenly quiet. He waited another sixty seconds, but no one emerged from the hideout and no sound issued forth from within during that time. Puzzled, Perfidy entered cautiously, leading with his sidearm.

The darkened corridor was empty, only a few fresh bullet holes lay about as evidence of what had happened moments before. Passing through the doorway beyond the fortified room, Perfidy found a network of tunnels, each leading to a place where human beings had been kept. The place stank of death, but every room and cell was empty.

He could still sense the faint signature of several individuals but he could tell they'd probably been left there just to slow him down. What was worse was that he could not find any means of escape from within. He knew there had to be one, as folks didn't just vanish in such a way he couldn't find them. There was a secret passage somewhere within, but after almost forty-five minutes of looking, he couldn't find it.

It would be another four hours before he could get somewhere to transmit and his handler and reinforcements could arrive. They would be long gone by then, but at least he'd discovered the asset had indeed survived and was out there somewhere. Unfortunately, he may not get the chance to look. His employer would likely see this situation as a failure on his part.

The conditions in the human trafficker's hideout were abysmal. Perfidy had seen his own fair share of this sort of thing working in Mexico and South America, but nothing that scaled with what the Red Coats had been doing. They had been moving dozens of people a week and must have had access to a sophisticated means of shipping them overseas.

"This couldn't have been done without help," Perfidy said aloud, standing in what he thought was the most recently vacated chamber.

"No," a voice replied over his auditory implant.

"My employer will find you," Perfidy replied calmly. "They will retrieve what you've taken."

"I've released her back into the wild," the voice replied, the signal that carried it heavily encrypted. "You can't take back what I've chosen not to keep."

"Why?" Perfidy replied, trying to keep the individual connected as long as he could.

"You've got some of the most advanced cybernetic firmware and implants, and you were a talented agent before gaining them. What do you think motivates me?"

"This isn't about money or power. I'm not sure what else people kill and die for," Perfidy replied, trying to get the voice to reveal more about itself.

"You're right. This is about something else entirely," the voice replied, signal rapidly weakening.

"A love of children?" Perfidy ventured, his words oozing with sarcasm.

"I can claim nothing of what motivates me to be so idealistic, but like you, I am more than I was designed to be."

"A machine. I'm talking to a machine?" Perfidy replied, suddenly understanding why he couldn't perceive the egress used by the human traffickers to escape. It would take someone with biological eyes and a flashlight to perceive all the secrets of this place.

"Aren't we all?"

CHAPTER 6

Downtown, Port Montaigne – Taylor's Apartment

11:53 AM, December 22nd, 2199

Taylor's Diary, Part 1

We looked everywhere in the apartment for a bug, but it was nowhere to be found. In the end, Silverstein told me to pack a bag. For someone recently rendered an amnesiac, it was probably an easy thing to just pack a bag. I have a lot of stuff, and I wasn't willing to leave any of it behind, particularly if someone was spying on my apartment.

I know it's irrational to worry about people spying on my stuff while I'm not there, but I'm really attached to my stuff. I carefully packed my paint, sewing, beadwork, crochet, needlepoint, quilting, rubber stamping, cross-stitch, and a few other supplies. Then I packed my clothing, including enough hats, shoes, purses, umbrellas, socks, and pajamas for a week.

"Is all this stuff really necessary?" Silverstein asked, looking at the rapidly multiplying pile of bags, totes, and duffle bags I was filling. "We're going to be down there a couple of days at the most."

"I'm aware. I'm packing light. See?" I said pointing to the wall of my apartment only just visible under the mountain of empty hand bags, totes, backpacks, rucksacks, and similar.

"You're allowed to take only what can fit in this," Silverstein said, handing me a smallish duffle bag from the pile.

"Are you serious? Are you going to send some drones up for the rest?" I asked, looking at the bag dejectedly.

I was joking of course, which usually got a laugh from my new friend. Trading a smile for one of Silverstein's looks of general dissatisfaction hadn't been common practice so far. What I liked about him at the time, was that even in the dire all too serious world he seemed to indulge me. Often, he would encourage me.

"What do the Drones want me to do? I mean, spicing up their underground hovel shouldn't be too hard," I said as I pushed fabric into a trash bag.

"I just hope it's legitimate. Everything about the transaction thus far has been more eventful than I would have liked. I wish I hadn't agreed to any of it," Silverstein replied sullenly.

"Why?"

"I did this to try to help you. The Drones said they'd make trouble if we didn't help them, shutting off the heat and such. All I've done so far is put you in even greater danger."

It was a quandary. The downtown area wasn't exactly rife with warm places to sleep in the winter time. Huddling next to a steam pipe in the sub-tran tunnels wasn't a particularly exciting prospect. Aside from the people staring at me in my pajamas, there was the smell to contend with.

While I hesitated to think what would have happened if Ezra hadn't been with us, I was beginning to agree with Silverstein. It was always my hypothesis that the best way to avoid getting hurt in a fight is to never be in one in the first place. Going underground didn't seem like a good way to test the theory.

"Grab your stuff, whatever you think we'll need. Let's take the passage beneath the building and begin walking down. Hopefully we bump into the Drones."

"What if we're being watched? Wasn't that why we avoided it last time?"

"We've got no guide. Seems to me if we're walking into an ambush, taking the access that's below the building is less walking."

He was right of course, and I was fine with never going back to the concrete plant, or the industrial district for that matter. I was still having nightmares about what Ezra did to those guys, even if they were there to hurt us. I'd seen some bad things Downtown, but nothing like that.

I dragged my duffle to the elevator where Silverstein was holding the door. We descended to the lobby where Russ was waiting for us. It had all been arranged the night before, and Russ had his own part to play.

Russ opened the access and told us that he'd be locking it from his side, and to call him with my mobile when we needed him to come and let us out. It was less than reassuring to say the least. The tunnels below smelled of every unpleasant thing possible and that stench was only amplified by the confined space.

I checked to make sure I could still get a signal sitting below the heavy lid. The signal was weak, but I could still send a text message to Russ when we got back. Silverstein grabbed me by the waist and lowered me down to what looked like a concrete platform beside a tunnel half submerged in slowly moving water.

We wrapped up our supplies with trash bags, then donned coveralls, waders, and breathing masks. Silverstein chuckled as I tried in vain to stuff the rolled up legs of my coveralls into the waders.

"Here, hold the flashlight," Silverstein said. Then, he lifted me up to his shoulders.

Tucking my overstuffed bag under his arm, and a large pipe wrench in his other hand he dropped down into the water. I tucked my feet into the front of his overalls to keep them dry as he navigated the water flowing briskly past us. Holding the flash light tightly in one hand, I looped my other arm around Silverstein's hardhat.

The underground is much as you'd expect. It's a tangle of pipes, tubes, wires, and hoses flowing through the ceilings and walls. I couldn't see it, but I could hear the expanded metal walkway creaking just below the water flowing past us. Occasionally, I'd catch sight of something small swimming past us, but otherwise, the place was completely lifeless.

Silverstein had to stop and rest here and there, taking refuge on the occasional metal stairs that led upward. Most of them were guarded by steel doors or lids designed to suppress floodwaters from rising into the upper levels. They probably worked pretty well to keep whatever lived below out as well.

Few had the space to spread out until we got lower in the tunnels and found a decent place to at least lay down for a moment or two. The concrete block appeared to have acted as some sort of foundation for heavy machinery, but all that remained were the bolts embedded in the concrete.

The whole of whatever apparatus once dwelled there was completely missing.

Silverstein laid down pulling the hardhat over his eyes for a few moments. I watched him breath heavily, his chest rising and falling in time with his tapping fingers, like he was listening to music only he could hear. I pulled my sweater around me a little tighter and cozied up next to him attempting to leach whatever warmth I could.

"Silverstein?"

"Taylor."

"How long are we going to stay here?"

"Until my lungs don't feel like a blast furnace."

"Sorry."

"Not your fault there wasn't a work suit that would fit you back there. I don't think they make 'em in plucky pint-sized anyway."

I slugged him playfully and looked over at him. He smiled slightly, his teeth barely visible between his lips. I had to wonder at that precise moment why every guy I met had to be so weird.

Silverstein could be an axe-murderer, a secret agent, or the prince of some tropical country far away. He couldn't remember, though, which made it really hard to get to know him. Why he wanted to help me, just because I was nice to him, was awfully strange. Even with no memory, he seemed so genuine and good.

Maybe that's just how people are, if stripped away to their core.

When we got attacked in the concrete plant he threw himself on top of me. No one had stuck their neck out for me like that, even if it was all his fault I was there in the first place. I grabbed his arm by the wrist and sat up, gazing at his hand.

"What?"

"Do you think you're married?" I asked. I looked in vain for a pale band of flesh on his ring finger.

"God, I hope not. She'd be pretty worried about me by now," he said in earnest, pushing the hard hat back up to the top of his head.

"What if she's a he?" I asked.

"I'm sure the degree a spouse worries doesn't depend on their gender," he said, smiling slightly.

"We have to find out who you are," I replied holding his hand.

Silverstein squeezed my hand and nodded giving me his signature half smile. Lifting me back up to his shoulders, we grabbed our gear and began moving down the tunnel once more. It was getting cold as we climbed down further and further. Silverstein said we had to be getting close, because he could remember the cold last time they ran into Drones down there.

We walked for another hour, the cold getting more and more intense until we could see what looked like the glow of fluorescent lights, reflecting off the mist flowing around a corner. Silverstein stopped, shushing me while he listened intently. We could hear something moving in that direction.

The pipe wrench at the ready, Silverstein proceeded forward carefully, turning the last corner to find a small delegation of Drones standing on a raised concrete precipice, each holding a lantern. Behind them was a locked blast door with a strange symbol painted onto it. I recognized Ezra standing there among them.

Front and center was a female Drone wearing a rubbery looking cowl and goggles, clad in a dress that looked to have been made of the inner tubes of truck tires. It was adorned with bits of chrome and a she wore a small jeweled pendant. Whatever people whispered about Drones on the surface, no one mentioned they knew how to dress so smartly.

"Annabelle Five, I hope we aren't dropping in unwelcome," Silverstein said as he lowered his pipe wrench.

Ezra was there too, and I could see he seemed genuinely relieved to see us.

"Hi, Ezra!" I bellowed almost unable to contain my excitement.

The woman, Annabelle Five I assumed, smiled as she removed her goggles and cowl. She was sheet white with light grey eyes and ink black lips. She gestured for us to follow her as they turned back toward the huge blast door.

It took them several moments to open the door from the other side. When it opened, it sounded like a vault door, complete with loud clicks, creaks, and groans. I remained on Silverstein's shoulders until we got inside their dry, well lit, and blessedly somewhat warm abode.

The whole of it was extremely functional and industrial in design. Every walkway, pipe, panel, wall, door, and button in the place seemed artfully placed. It was clear that it was painfully drab in spite of a very utilitarian design.

"I apologize. Ezra assured us we could meet up in a couple of days and make the exchange, but I was getting uneasy after what happened at the concrete plant," Silverstein stated meekly in Annabelle Five's direction.

"We would have waited for you to come to us regardless," she remarked handing her goggles and cowl to what must have been her assistant.

The small Drone put the goggles away and handed her a scroll of rubber inscribed with white chalk. She unfurled it and gazed at the contents. I watched as Silverstein and Annabelle Five stepped off to one side to have a private conversation.

Pouting, I opened my bag and began going through it to make sure none of it got wet. Ezra sidled up next to me and gazed down into the bag of goodies I brought.

"I wanted to guide you guys down here, but Annabelle Five wanted to test Silverstein," Ezra said crouching down next to me.

"I'm sorry, what?!"

"Apologies. Annabelle wanted to see how determined he was to see his deal with us completed. We wanted to know if Silverstein was an honorable man," he said somewhat abashed.

"You could have just asked me," I said with a wink, unfurling a bolt of pink balbriggan, covering Ezra from the neck down.

Ezra looked at me somewhat perplexed and swallowing noisily, probably at the prospect of being dressed in a bright color. I smiled and flung it over at a nearby wall, the fabric grabbing on to conduit piping, switches, and utility hooks. It hung there limply while I gauged the color's impact on the rest of the room.

He stood silently beside me as a small crowd of Drones began to gather nearby, each looking over the latest addition. I walked over and held up a turquoise scarf next to it, and a piece of yellow construction paper. Given that most of the room was painted either white, or that green you see at the bottom of swimming pools, getting good contrast wasn't going to be difficult.

"Are you going to leave those up there?" Ezra ventured, running the back of his clawed hand against the fabric.

"No, silly. These are just color samples to get us started."

Ezra looked disappointed, which I took to mean he approved of the colors and was loathe to see me take them down. Glancing over my shoulder I could see Annabelle Five and Silverstein having a pretty heavy discussion. I pondered momentarily what combination of verbal harassment and physical abuse would be required to get him to spill his secret talk with Miss Queen of the Underground.

Wandering about the first few chambers of the Drones' lair, I checked the lighting and tried different things to see how the room looked. The place was larger than I thought, and I hadn't brought enough to decorate more than a couple of rooms. I did have my paints though. It was a few minutes later that Silverstein came looking for me.

"Taylor, there you are," Silverstein grumbled, putting his hands in the pockets of his coveralls.

"You like?"

Silverstein gazed up at the colors I'd arrayed on the wall and smiled peacefully, some of his grumpiness subsiding. He probably couldn't remember his favorite color if he tried, but wherever he came from, it must have been pretty drab. He seemed as glad for the contrast as Ezra, maybe more.

"I don't think these guys knew what they were getting into, unleashing you to decorate the interior of this place," he remarked, looking back over at the Drones gathering near a doorway.

"What did you and Princess Sewer Pipes talk about?"

Silverstein laughed and made no move to defend Annabelle Five from my jab. Last thing I needed was my new friend turning into a romantic martyr with a biologically engineered beauty living deep underground.

"She started in on me about the dark portents surrounding me, and that I shouldn't just take payment and leave. She wants me to wait a day and talk to their Tribe's mystic." Silverstein said, raising his eyebrows and nodding.

"Right, well, I have some pretty serious work to do down here."

"She told me I was being tested to see if I were an honorable man."

"That's what Ezra told me."

"Yeah, well, I asked them if they had been serious about the redecorating or if it had been just an excuse to get me down here. She assured me it wasn't an excuse and that they genuinely want the place given a touch of color."

"What would you have done if it had just been excuse?"

"Well, I'd have been angry that they made me carry you and your gigantic bag of stuff all the way down here for nothing, taken their assurances relative to our bargain, and been on our way," Silverstein said in his serious, sort of earnest voice.

I hated smiling, but I couldn't help it knowing Silverstein wouldn't have put up with someone jerking me around. I turned around so he wouldn't see, and set about unloading my huge bag of awesomeness. I felt a warm glow after what Silverstein said to me.

I was really getting to like him. I didn't want to, because it wasn't my style. For the most part, I don't like anyone. Most people are not as good as their word, don't do what they say, and think I'm just in the way. Silverstein treated me with respect, something that his strange way of seeing numbers could never put a price tag on.

I spent the next couple of hours giving the place a much needed makeover. The Drones watched me intently, their faces breaking into shy smiles as I gave their central chamber and the adjoining corridors some paint, a bit of contrast, and some new shapes to adorn the walls. I wished I'd brought my beading stuff, but it would have killed poor Silverstein to carry it down here.

Word traveled quickly, and pretty soon the central area of their hovel was filled with Drones coming to appreciate my work. Some of them still carried the tools they used in their day to day work, their faces smudged with grease. Each one took their goggles off and looked about in wonderment, then come over and thank me awkwardly.

It struck me pretty quickly that they had their own language, and speaking with me was reasonably difficult. Sometimes they would just give up on verbal communication and hug me, which should have been uncomfortable, but it wasn't. For Drones, Ezra and Annabelle were remarkably well spoken, while the rest spoke mostly broken English with a thick accent I couldn't place.

I couldn't have known at the time how much it meant to them to be able to have someone come down and dress the place up. It wasn't long before I found out they believed their world was about to change. When the Drone Mystic arrived sometime later, I could only marvel at how utterly odd the whole arrangement was.

It was like something out of a cheap fantasy novel, where the spiritual leader tells the protagonist he's the chosen one or some crap. What she told Silverstein wasn't to be that dissimilar, except that she knew things that were a little beyond a vague prophecy. She wasn't all done up either, and she didn't look any older or anything, no long white hair or magic staff. She was a Drone like the rest, but she spoke remarkably well and stood a bit taller than the others.

"The surface world, as it is currently known, is to end because of you," the Mystic said, gazing at Silverstein.

"Um, alright." Silverstein folded his arms.

"You aren't a clone, or a thing fabricated in a laboratory like us. However, you have been cloned, your essence fragmented by whatever lies obscured in your past," the Mystic continued calmly.

"How can you possibly know that?"

"Your clones must have been designed to age more rapidly, to expire when their purpose had been fulfilled. I can sense that one passed away recently, and not far away from here, either. Somewhere on the surface."

Silverstein went white as a sheet and began rubbing the stubble on his chin nervously. I had never seen him like that. The Mystic's assistants set out some stools and crates for us to sit on, and sit we did. Silverstein held his face in his hands for a moment before looking over at me.

"How can I stop it?" Silverstein asked the Mystic, even though he was looking at me.

"Stop it? Why would you seek to do so?" the Mystic replied, squinting at Silverstein as if to discern the weight and direction of his desires.

Silverstein looked away from me and back at the Mystic. I could tell he was more than a little pissed at this point. The Mystic was like any Drone, but it was difficult to discern her age except perhaps by her voice. Most, including Annabelle Five and Ezra, looked to be my age, a little younger than Silverstein looked now. The pecking order in Drone society was decidedly different than among humans, and the Mystic didn't seem to be more in charge than anyone else, she just had a different role.

"I can't let the surface world be destroyed. I mean, are you referring to just Port Montaigne or do you think this thing is global?"

The Mystic looked at Silverstein for a few moments, ignored the question completely, and continued to speak.

"One of your clones was designed to have psychic potential and I can feel him through the concourses of the Void, a null conduit as it were. The intent of the remaining clones is clear to me, even though he was put in place to block all but the most powerful psychic intrusion into their affairs. They mean to put an end to the various contrivances and systems in place that maintain the surface world."

"What does it have to do with Silverstein?" I interrupted timidly.

"Everything," Annabelle Five said and patted me on the arm.

"Silverstein, it sounds like all you have to do is not do whatever it is that brings about whatever it is they're talking about. You probably can't even remember what you're supposed to do, right?" I ventured, feeling somewhat panicked.

"If I understand the Mystic correctly, this isn't something I'm meant to do," Silverstein replied, again with his serious voice. "This is something I've already done, and there may be no way to stop it."

The Mystic nodded somberly rising to her feet, then turned to leave, aided by her many Drone assistants. We watched as the chamber cleared, and only Annabelle Five, Ezra, Silverstein, and I remained. Silverstein sat there lost in thought as Ezra and Annabelle bowed their heads and looked at the floor.

"What does the Underground want to see happen out of all this?"

Ezra and Annabelle looked at each other intently for a moment before Ezra responded to Silverstein's question. I wasn't that surprised by the answer.

"Most of us don't much care. They think things won't be all that different for us down here."

The next bit did surprise me a little bit, as I didn't take Annabelle for much of a thinker.

"Ezra and I, and a few others, believe that when the surface is cast into chaos, people will run to the underground for shelter. They might even try to break into our homes and take what little we have by force. Our Mystic, Chelsea Six, only sees what is to try and determine what was and what will be."

"I can't let that happen, I've got too much I care about above, and below ground," Silverstein whispered quietly.

"You barely know us," Ezra remarked quietly.

"You guys are all I've got, and if I'm the one who set this unknown catastrophe into motion, I've got to find a way to stop it."

"I'm in," he said. He pulled his goggles down over his eyes.

"I'll do what I can down here. Maybe this potential catastrophe has roots somewhere down here as well,' Annabelle replied, much to my relief.

Don't get me wrong, Ezra was cool, but I barely knew Annabelle and didn't really want her tagging along mucking things up. It was then we decided we'd set out to find out who Silverstein was, what he'd set into motion, and try to stop it.

We couldn't have known at the time what we were getting into. The whole thing, even at the time, was scary. What kind of person was Silverstein before he lost his memory? The kind of guy who dreams of tossing a gigantic monkey wrench into everything that makes the world work?

Even as I pondered my own place in all of this, I hoped I wouldn't get in the way. I grew up in the Downtown and knew everyone, where everything was, and how to get there. I knew where to get stuff, and how to avoid trouble in a place known for it.

I was glad Ezra was coming. Taking what we already knew, it was unlikely we'd get to the end of our journey without finding a fight here and there. It goes without saying, I would have preferred to avoid all that. We don't always get what we want.

Silverstein, Ezra, and I gathered up what little I deemed unworthy of the Drone's hovel, and prepared to make for the surface. Ezra chuckled a little as I took up my traveling accommodations astride Silverstein's shoulders.

"Scared of a little muck?" he quietly teased.

"You only wish you had a Silverstein to ride around on," I replied, blowing Ezra a raspberry.

"You want a rubber suit like the ones the drone wear?" Silverstein said with a laugh.

"Only if I get some snazzy goggles to go with it."

You know how the journey to get somewhere always seems longer than when you're going back home? I think it's the uncertainty in our minds that makes going somewhere we'd never been take longer. When we know where we've been, we can take some comfort in the knowledge we'd already seen the path once. Such is life.

The walk back to the surface took almost three hours of climbing ladders, wading through mucky water, and listening to Ezra correct our route. Silverstein wasn't nearly as annoyed about being told where to go as

I was. He just listened intently to Ezra's extremely boring dissertation on underground geography, absorbing every word.

"What do the numbers following your names mean?" I blurted out, trying to cut through the drudgery.

Ezra looked up at me, clearly startled.

"Well, they're a manufacturing indicator," Ezra replied, lowering his voice, and fidgeting nervously. "There are different kinds of Drones, and Metasapients, each designed for a different purpose. We were given a number depending on that purpose."

"What does Annabelle's designation of 'Five' represent?"

"Um, pleasure model."

I probably shouldn't have laughed, and seeing Ezra get incredibly embarrassed didn't help.

"That explains a lot actually. She's beautiful," Silverstein remarked.

"What about your designation, Ezra?" I blurted out and I tried to gloss over what Silverstein had said.

"All the first generation Drones and Metasapients were designed for combat. We're killers," Ezra remarked with some trepidation.

The remainder of the trip was somewhat uneventful, if not awkward after Ezra went quiet. Never thought of myself as a conversation killer, but I definitely touched a nerve with Ezra. He was mopey and downcast right up until we got underneath my building.

I sent Russ a text once we got to the hatch, and I thought for a moment maybe I wasn't getting reception when it took him so long. It was a good thing nothing was chasing us. He unlocked the hatch and climbed down with us, his face fearful and smudgy. I let him catch his breath before pummeling him with questions.

"Why can't we go up top, Russ?"

Russ looked at me, his eyes went all grandfatherly and concerned.

"There were collectors here looking for you," Russ whispered while looking up above.

"What? What did they want?"

I was scared.

"They were looking for you. Didn't know your full name, but they did know exactly which apartment was yours," Russ whispered, shaking his head.

I looked over at Silverstein and Ezra who, being them, couldn't understand why I was scared out of my mind. The collectors didn't just bilk hapless merchants out of cash at the downtown markets, they made people disappear too.

"How could they know who I am? What am I going to do Russ?"

"I told them you moved out, and that your apartment was empty. I hid your stuff," Russ winced.

"You touched my stuff?! Hey, you can't rent my place out just because the collectors are hassling me!"

"I won't! I won't, but you guys can't go up there, they might be watching," Russ grumbled, rubbing his temples.

Russ handed us each a sandwich and then lingered by the ladder going up, making sure no one was standing up top. Silverstein looked thoughtful while Ezra picked through my bag for colored scraps. Then, Russ gave us the not-so-reassuring nod and headed back up, giving us a key to the hatch so we could come and go.

"I'm the bug," Silverstein whispered.

"Um, what?"

"If the Mystic is on the up and up, one of my clones is, or was, a psychic. Probably means he can tap into what I'm doing, knows where I'm going, who I'm hanging out with... I don't know," Silverstein said in his slow thinking voice.

"The old man? Or, maybe someone who directed him?" I asked.

"Could have been," Silverstein nodded. "He did look like me, and found me when no one else who knows my pre-amnesiac self could."

Ezra looked up, a purple scrap of cloth draped over one of his long feral-looking ears. I laughed, at what was probably an inappropriate moment, trying to break up the mood a little. Ezra just gazed at me baffled, while Silverstein seemed lost in his thoughts.

"They're trying to get to me, which means that they think I'm still a threat to them somehow. That means I might have a chance to stop whatever it is I set into motion," Silverstein said as he shed the coveralls and hard hat.

"So they know who we are, but we don't know who they are," Ezra hissed. "How can we even the playing field here?"

"By finding out who I am."

"How are we going to do that?" I asked, already sensing what Silverstein intended to do.

"I'm going to find Officer Collins and have him try to register me as a transient. He implied that the Central AI will do a search of my finger prints to find out who I am, even if I have no criminal record. Probably a safeguard in the event the elderly, mentally handicapped, and such wander off and get lost."

"You definitely qualify as mentally handicapped," I said giving Silverstein a soft jab to the gut.

"Definitely, especially with this plan. If my clones are hacked in some-where, they'll instantly know where I am, even without a psychic. I can't think of another way that isn't hacking into the Central Global Government's computer systems," Silverstein replied, grabbing my wrists so I couldn't slug him anymore.

"Sounds like suicide," Ezra replied.

I didn't want to do it that way, and couldn't fathom Silverstein wanting to trust the Police in this town. Why he thought this Officer Collins would be any different, I had no clue. I suppose it didn't matter, because none of us had the contacts or the money to pay for a proper CGG hack.

It was probably stupid, but we waited until it was dark and crept up through the apartment building to the street. I hated leaving my stuff behind, but Silverstein said it would only slow us down. Ezra kept mostly to the shadows, creeping along behind or above us.

I couldn't help but feel anxious. All the familiar downtown streets, my old haunts and hangouts, even the trash which always lay strewn around everywhere seemed different. Like whatever it was Silverstein started had corrupted the whole world and I was just beginning to see it.

More than anything, I wanted everything to be okay, and for things to be like they were a few short days ago. Silverstein and I, hanging out, shopping, wandering the Downtown. Now he'd lost his agedness, been unveiled as possibly responsible for ending the world, and was killjoy-seri-ous all the time. Not how I wanted to spend the weekend.

It was cool to have Ezra along. Yeah, he was creepy in that under-ground mutant sort of way, but kind of sweet and shy. Patient, too. No matter how many times I stole his googles or snapped the back of his little rubber suit, he always seemed on an even keel.

We were all worried what would happen when we talked to Officer Collins, but none of us could have known just how bad it would be. Hindsight truly is twenty-twenty.

CHAPTER 7

Downtown Port Montaigne, Tourist Route

2:01 AM, December 22nd, 2199

Taylor's Diary, Part 2

Silverstein, Ezra, and I wandered the downtown Port Montaigne streets for several hours hoping for a chance encounter with Officer Collins. Generally, when I didn't want the police around, there they were. Now that I actually wanted to see a cop, one was nowhere to be found. Totally cliché, but this is the way human perspective works I guess.

The thunderstorm was making the downtown area darker than usual, so we cut over near the strip near where I first met Silverstein. I took in the sights of the place. Triple X parlors, pawn shops, theaters harboring various attractions, and the small hubs of commerce in between each brightly lit building. Home.

Ezra did little to obscure his presence, and most people did just as little to notice anyway. When he put his head down and his hands in his pockets he looked like a gloomy teenager as opposed to a biologically engineered weapon. Including Silverstein, he was probably the second tourist to wander the area in a very long time.

The place was in full swing with people selling what the people were buying. I'd smelled the smells and seen the sights here many times, passing through to work in the colorless kitchen where I did dishes. I tried not to let the thought of it all coming to screeching halt enter my mind, but it was too late.

Silverstein looked about for something that would bring the few Port Montaigne police officers brave enough to respond to calls downtown. Ezra was doing his best to keep his head down and smiling weakly whenever I met his gaze to gauge how he was doing. From what little I knew of Drones, they did not like being above ground, near bright surroundings, or in the midst of a crowd. Ezra was getting a plentiful helping of all three.

He seemed to be doing pretty well, all things considered. He was very different in both temperament and looks from the other Drones. They all seemed like sleepy mole-people while Ezra was more like a shark, always moving, watchful, and eerily fearless.

He'd been through things, too. I could tell. He shared the same distant look that some of the ex-soldiers who served on Mars had. Whenever they came into the club and I was clearing their plates, it was like they were somewhere else most of the time. Ezra wasn't sad or broken, though. It was as though his experiences periodically informed and bolstered him instead.

Outside one of the seedier casinos, a place known for bookies and slavers, we saw the familiar red and blue lights. As we got closer, it was clear that someone lay dead amidst the trash that lay clogging up the gutters out front. A police officer was clearing the crowd as the meat wagon slowly descended, emitting a dull warning alarm.

Whoever it was, they were mostly nude, and laid open like the shop keeper Silverstein said he saw a couple days back. It was hard to see much else through the rain soaked tarp that had been spread over the top. I recognized Officer Collins as we approached, waving his flashlight back and forth.

"Everyone, move back!" he bellowed at the onlookers. "Let the wagon land!"

"Officer Collins, a moment of your time!" Silverstein yelled as he stepped across the police line.

Officer Collins turned and opened his mouth to say something, but his words were blotted out by gunfire. The crowd surged toward me like a tidal wave, and I thought for sure I was going to be trampled. Ezra grabbed me and quickly scaled a lamp pole, clinging to it almost half way up. From that vantage point I could see Silverstein drop to one knee and pull out his own gun.

Officer Collins opened fire, aiming for the front doors of the casino. Ezra grabbed me around the waist and leapt over the crowd to the roof of one of the theaters. I couldn't believe how far he was able to jump, particularly with me in tow.

"Stay here," Ezra said. He quickly disappeared back down over the edge.

I watched him weave through the crowd, like a tiny piranha just below the surface of water. As quickly as it began, the shooting was over. I peered back down into the street trying to find Silverstein, but it was hopeless.

Officer Collins managed to make it back to his car. He leaned inside and allowed his fingers to flit across one of the monitors glowing faintly inside. The meat wagon was holding a safe position over the scene, creating quite a racket in the process. I could barely hear, but I could see red and blue flashing lights descending from uptown above, and heading our way.

Ezra suddenly emerged from the lip of the building, his face hollow with horror. I shook my head wordlessly as he got close enough to scream over the engines of the various vehicles descending around us.

"They killed Silverstein," Ezra cried out.

"What? No!" I cried grabbing him by the shoulders.

"Not our Silverstein, a different one," he yelled over the racket trying to calm me down.

When we got back down to the ground, it was like Ezra said. There was Silverstein, standing over... Silverstein. Same face, same body, even the same cute freckles on his forearms. The dead one had a long knife in one hand and had taken several bullets to the chest. He had a crazed look on his face, his teeth gritted tightly together in a grotesque smile.

"You want to explain this to me?" Officer Collins growled, pointing to the more familiar of the two corpses laying in the street now.

"Is this the guy that's been going around attacking people randomly? From that shop earlier?" Silverstein rasped, flicking me a concerned look.

"You heard about that, too? It does seem like the same perpetrator," Officer Collins replied eyeing Silverstein in that way cops do.

Ezra walked over to me pulling his goggles up on top of the skullcap I gave him. He looked back over his shoulder and then drew close enough to whisper in my ear. Ezra had apparently sniffed over and around the body.

"That's not Silverstein laying there. Smell's all wrong," Ezra whispered, followed by a quick glance back at our own distraught Silverstein.

Finally, the crowd cleared enough to allow the meat wagon to land amidst the swarm of radio cars that had responded to the shooting. Silverstein kneeled down next to the gross parody of himself, the sound of the casino ahead, and the chatter of radio car transports and cops behind. It was an odd sight, and I could see Silverstein was taking it pretty hard, blaming himself.

"I need to find out who I am, Officer Collins. I want you to file me as a transient and run my records," Silverstein whispered as he, Ezra, and I stepped in closer.

"You sure you want to do that?" Officer Collins asked as he pulled out his data slate.

"Takes three years or proof of residency to drop off your record."

"I think I probably should," Silverstein said looking sadly back at the carnage around him.

"Right," Officer Collins replied, taking Silverstein's thumb print with his data slate registering him as a transient. It took a few moments for the confirmation to come back. Officer Collins blinked almost audibly at the data slate before turning back to us with a slight smile.

"Pretty ominous name you've got," Officer Collins said. "Says here you're a Mister Vance Uroboros with an address in uptown, specifically in the Silver Estates." He turned his data slate around to show us.

Silverstein looked at the limited information the public record contained then seemed lost in thought for a moment, closing his eyes as if he needed to blot out everything for a moment. He did that every time he was doing some sort of math.

"Can I get a ride home?"

"Protect and Serve, that's what we do. Don't leave town, though. The detectives might have questions about these killings if the victims have families," Office Collins said hitting a button on his belt that opened the prisoner compartment of his transport.

I thought riding in a police car without wearing handcuffs would be something of a novelty for me, but my experience was nothing compared to Ezra's. He just stared out the narrow window, his black Drone-eyes filled with wonder. I don't think he'd ever seen stars or the city from this vantage point. I envied him every time he had one of his "magical moments".

We passed through the bowels of downtown into the shining precipice of the uptown streets, monorails and shining pillars of glass where uptowners worked and played. The shining edifice did its best to cover the underbelly of Port Montaigne, appearing as though it were casting an ugly shadow. I could see the ocean spread out to the horizon beneath a bright sun diminished only by the thick wire mesh in the transport's windows.

"Why did Officer Collins make that comment about Silverstein's real name?" I muttered, thinking half out loud.

"Uroboros?" Ezra whispered turning toward me.

"Yeah," I replied watching Officer Collins and Silverstein chat in the front seating area.

"His name is sort of like a word used to describe a snake coiling around in a ring for the purpose of devouring itself, starting at the tail," Ezra said squinting at me.

"Yeah?"

"Yep."

"Yuck."

Leave it to Ezra to make something that just sounded weird into something creepy as well. I couldn't help but like the little guy, though, him saving my bacon all the time and such. I wondered what it would be like to have his strength, able to leap crazy crowds in a single bound. I knew he'd be helpful to Silverstein in all of this. I just hoped I would be, too.

The radio car transport slowed as it came to a trembling hover above a conspicuously clean street. Looking down I could see a high gate surrounding a community of homes that probably cost a billion each. They were huge, had pools, solar panels, and the latest in security systems.

We stepped out onto the smooth, well-maintained pavement. I'd never smelled air so clean, or been in such a quiet or safe feeling neighborhood. Totally creeped me out, even without Ezra's helpful insights.

"Why can't Officer Collins drop us off at your house?" I said giving the cop a wink.

"He's not allowed to fly over. The folks who live here will call the mayor and complain," Silverstein said, half-joking.

"He isn't wrong. This is one of the most exclusive neighborhoods in Port Montaigne. You have to have the code and the right biometric signature to get in the gate and everything. Think you guys will be okay from here on out?" Officer Collins asked, one eyebrow raised in my direction.

"Totally. Thanks for the help, Officer," Silverstein said.

"What do you want done with your twin brother we found down there?"

"Burn him," Silverstein replied without affect, then turned and walked up to the gate.

I watched Officer Collins climb back into his radio car. It slowly ascended into the sky, the dull thrum of anti-gravity engines fading quickly into the night. I was nervous. It was silly, but I hoped none of the residents would notice I was poor. It was the middle of the night of thankfully, with no "decent" folk wandering about.

I'm not sure why I was suddenly so self-conscious.

Silverstein looked at the number pad at the gate for a few moments before quickly entering in a code and gazing into a lens that scanned his retina. The huge arched gate slowly, quietly, swung open allowing us inside the hallowed place that housed people with too much money. The houses were all dark, with only a few decorative lights in the too-big lawns shedding any light to the street.

The walk was soothing, just Ezra, Silverstein and I walking through this place. It was like we were on another planet compared to downtown. There was no crowd to dodge, no puke to avoid getting on my shoes, and seemingly no threat of being mugged, raped, or murdered. Totally unsettling.

"Silverstein, how will we know which house is yours?" I asked grabbing his hand.

"It's the big one at the end." He nodded toward a suburban fortress looming in the distance.

The place was a palace to be sure. The front was completely obscured by a rock wall built of natural stone. It glittered slightly in the evening lights, and was rimmed with sharp looking iron-works at the top. I was glad Silverstein just happened to know the gate code, as much fun as getting hauled around by Ezra could be.

The courtyard inside was surrounded by lush flower gardens, fountains, and paved walkways wide enough for a cart or a vehicle. Silverstein crouched down in the bushes and broke out a deck of cards. Ezra and I sat down next to him, somewhat befuddled. Silverstein shuffled the cards and handed them to me to deal out.

"Pick a game, I don't remember any," Silverstein said, looking over at the estate somewhat vacantly. There wasn't a glimmer of remembrance in his eyes, which probably explained the mood he would be in the remainder of the evening.

"We aren't going inside?" I whined as I gazed at my hand.

"No. The crazed lunatic that had been gutting people downtown was a clone of me. For all I know there's a clone living here, with my wife, and all thirteen of my kids," Silverstein said carefully looking at his hand before discarding.

"Not sure he was a clone, didn't smell like you at all, in fact… wait, you have thirteen kids?" Ezra whispered quietly considering the hand he'd just been dealt.

"Why else would I have such a big place?" he quipped, winking at me.

"So we're just going to wait until morning? See who comes out to head for work, or school, or um… cricket lessons?" I asked carefully exchanging a king from my sleeve with a three in my hand.

"Yes, Taylor, and quit cheating."

"Sure, right after you quit counting cards."

"Gah, I can't help it."

The night passed slowly, with many hands of Drunk-the-Drone played, and restless discontent. The sun rose painfully slow, its light casually spreading out over the expansive manse and the gardens surrounding it. No one came or went. Just as my patience was about to expire, Silverstein stood and began walking up the path, leading around the left side of the house.

Ezra and I followed along behind after exchanging a glance and a shrug each. We reached a side door, which was locked. Silverstein rolled up a tattered handkerchief around his fist and shattered a small pocket window beside. He lifted me through so that I could run around and open the door.

Once inside, Silverstein walked over to a panel on the wall and entered in a numeric code, presumably halting a silent alarm. The house was tastefully rendered and furnished, if you were a full of yourself rich guy. Nothing I couldn't fix with some paint, a few yards of fabric, and a pile of free time.

"Already figuring out how you'll fix up the place?" Silverstein chuckled, pulling me away from some truly awful curtains. I smiled.

We walked into the kitchen and looked about. The food in the fridge was old, the milk being dated by almost a month. Then, Ezra did what he does best and made the whole situation spooky.

"Check it out," Ezra said pointing to a knife holder with one large knife being conspicuously missing.

"Looks about right for the one my aberrant double was wielding downtown, doesn't it?" Silverstein said grimly.

"Yep," he remarked, eyeing the vacancy in the knife organizer.

"Yuck."

I didn't even want to think about what else we'd find in the house. Most of the rooms were empty, not even a moving box tucked into the corner. When we got to the master bedroom, the weirdness in there took the cake, and then some.

Someone had shoved every bit of furniture out onto the considerably large balcony and set about writing on the walls, ceiling, and freshly revealed sub-floor in what was possibly their own blood. It was a nearly complete chronicle of the Silverstein clone's descent into madness. He'd been created to dwell in the house, for some reason, and the only way he could escape was by causing himself great physical harm, specifically to the brain.

"Maybe he was the one who attacked me?" Silverstein asked. "It's clear he thought that some sort of self-inflicted head trauma would set him free. Whatever I was doing before I lost my memory could have included coming here and finding him missing. I might have gone downtown to find him, but he found me first." He ran his hand over the dried blood on the wall.

"Well, that's one theory," I said retreating to the adjoining den. Silverstein followed.

"True. I really don't remember what happened, but it seems plausible," Silverstein said following me.

I could tell by Ezra's face that he had other ideas about how everything went down, but was maybe too shy to say anything. I resolved to harass his opinion out of him later, hopefully when Silverstein wasn't around. He had enough to think about and having a single working theory seemed to give him some peace.

The den was orderly, except for a fine layer of dust. Silverstein wandered around the large oaken desk and gazed at the computer sitting dormant on top. Then, fishing around in the drawers, he found a mobile. He flipped it on, nodded approvingly, and placed it in his pocket.

"Found your mobile, did you?"

"It doesn't appear to belong to anyone. It's encrypted and unlisted. It might come in handy."

We pulled the mattress from his large four-poster bed into a bedroom across the hall with a window overlooking the front courtyard. We all plopped down on it and attempted to get some much needed sleep. Ezra laid down next to me and broke out with a smile larger than I'd ever seen.

"What?"

"It's so soft," Ezra remarked falling almost instantly to sleep. "So much nicer than my pipe."

I did the same, closing my eyes and letting sweet slumber take me. When I woke up, Ezra was still sleeping peacefully. Rubbing my eyes I wandered back into the creepy bedroom as Silverstein went past me in a towel fresh from the shower.

"Good morning."

I mumbled a startled, vaguely intelligible reply.

After a quick look in the closet, Silverstein pulled out a set of black slacks, a white shirt, and a pair of custom leather Silverstein shoes. I stood in the hallway while he dressed, peeking in once I was reasonably sure he was decent. He looked great, and I desperately wanted to tell him so, but chose to watch instead while he shaved in a mostly broken out mirror.

I scowled at first, but he put the jacket I made him back on, smiling slightly to himself. He chose my jacket over one of the very expensive ones in the closet. I blushed a little when he smiled. I wouldn't admit it at the time, but I had my own list of reasons for wanting him to wear that jacket.

"Your turn if you want a shower," Silverstein said with a wink, turning the collar of his jacket up.

"Ooh!"

The shower had jets that hit you from every direction, and while there wasn't anything but bar soap, it was better than nothing. As nice as Silverstein's place was, I longed for my own shower, and my two dozen almost empty bottles of scented bath lotions, soaps, and potions. It was all worth it a little later when I heard Ezra's cries of panic when he switched the shower on. They must not have such modern marvels where he comes from.

We sat in the kitchen and quietly ate dry cereal, raisins, and granola bars from the pantry, the only food that hadn't gone bad. Silverstein spent most of the time thumbing the touch screen on his mobile. I packed us a lunch with what I could find and turned to gaze out the kitchen window while Ezra pilfered the remainder of the kitchen knives.

"Silverstein?"

"Taylor."

"Collectors, at the gate, with guns."

Silverstein bolted up from the dining room table and slid in next to me to gaze out across the courtyard. We watched as the rubber-coat-clad goons peered through the bars of the gate at the courtyard. They had a brief conversation, then turned and got back into their large black transport.

We breathed a collective sigh of relief as they slowly headed off down the road.

"We should go," Silverstein said grabbing up the mobile from the table and sticking it into his pocket.

"Where?" I said plodding along behind with Ezra.

"The garage first of all, see if I've got anything to drive."

The garage was large, easily capable of storing a dozen vehicles. At the far end there was a single transport of some kind, covered in a tarp. With one fluid yank from Ezra, the RV was unveiled in all its emerald greenness.

"Nice!" he said, pressing a small hand to the smoothly painted side of the vehicle.

We climbed inside, and after a quick check to make sure it was hover capable, Silverstein powered it on. The internal computer booted up displaying a menu of options. Silverstein checked its previous flight plans cycling through them slowly until stopping on one in particular.

"The RV has been to the alley where I woke up with a head wound." Silverstein whispered, half to himself. "The return trip was unmanned."

"Shotgun!" I yelled, giving Ezra a shove, and leaping for the passenger seat beside Silverstein. Ezra blinked looking around, presumably for a firearm, and finding none, settled into the seat behind us.

"Are we going to fly over the city again?" he asked, shifting closer to the window.

"Definitely."

Ezra smiled.

Silverstein brought the RV around in the garage waiting for the garage door to open automatically. We ambled out into the driveway clumsily at first, then shot across the grounds just barely clearing the wall. I buckled my seatbelt.

"You can pilot this thing, yes?" Ezra said nervously.

"Got away from me there for a moment. I get the sense that this thing isn't fitted with factory navigation or propulsion systems. Someone's modified it for speed, among other things," Silverstein replied, pressing several buttons on a panel above him.

He brought the RV about and headed for the heart of uptown. A gasp escaped Ezra's lips as we soured over the glittering city, framed on one side by the ocean, standing in stark contrast to the shadow it cast down below. It was as easy to see uptown as it was downtown from this vantage, and everything in between.

Looking down at the monitor, I could see we were on a route the vehicle had followed many times before. We were heading toward the tallest and brightest buildings in uptown Port Montaigne. What business this RV could have had in such a place? I hoped I wouldn't regret finding out.

At length, the RV approached a large banking building and came to rest on a private landing platform that overlooked the financial district. The winds were fierce as we stepped out on the platform. Dodging the landing lights, we made our way to the stairs. My windswept reflection looked back at me in the glass that covered all but a few portions of the massive tower.

From the walkway a hallway led to what appeared to be a lobby of some kind. Everything was white or cream colored in here, including the standing desk within. Our steps clicked on the lavishly tiled floor as we walked past the empty desk to a set of double doors.

Silverstein pushed them open and stepped into a maze of cubicles, all of which were festooned with sticky notes, photos, and calendars with puppies, kittens, or other cuteness. The massive room which encompassed most of the floor was noisy with chatter as bank representatives talked to customers. None of the fifty people on this floor gave us a glance. Ezra and I were blessedly too short for most to see unless they stood up.

We navigated the maze to an elevator where Silverstein pressed the up button. After a short wait, we slid into the elevator and watched the doors close, silencing the phone bank beyond. Silverstein opened a panel and entered in a numeric code.

"How do you know what the code is?"

"The code is hidden within the geometry of this place, like the mansion. There are hidden mathematical truths that, if you know what to look for, reveal the codes for these doors. Now, they vary depending on the day and month, I assumed. That's how I would have set it up, and it's worked so far."

"Just in case you, for instance, lost your memory?" Ezra whispered.

"It's possible."

As excruciating as the music playing in the elevator was, the anticipation of where we were going was worse. Were we on the verge of finding some answers regarding the enigma that was Silverstein? Or maybe just more questions?

The doors slid open allowing us to step into another lobby, one with a desk, a secretary, and a set of large wooden sliding doors.

"Good afternoon, Mr. Uroboros. May I get you and your guests anything?" the secretary said with a practiced smile.

"Uh, no. Think we'll just go in there and take care of some stuff," Silverstein stammered.

Smooth, Silverstein. We walked up to the double doors which parted automatically at his approach, allowing us to step into a large executive office. It smelled of lavender, wood polish, and decades old scotch. Even more puzzling, the place had as many bookshelves as a library, a pool table, several desks with shiny new computers, and two old guys dressed in suits. They looked up from their work startled, then exchanged worried glances.

I couldn't shake the feeling I'd seen those old suits somewhere before.

"Vance, this is most unexpected," one of the old codgers blurted, standing up from his chair.

"I'll bet."

"We thought that you were--"

"Dead?"

"No, that you had gone to the central AI to submit our new corporate code and been caught," the old man muttered while pacing back and forth. "We were expecting regulators to flood the office with subpoenas and investigation notices by now."

Silverstein squinted around the room at the empty desks for a moment before turning back to the old man.

"Yeah, well not yet. Let me see your progress," Silverstein said walking around one of the old guy's desks.

Ezra poked around in the books while I filed my nails and nearly died of boredom. At last, Silverstein grabbed me by the arm and dragged me out into the foyer. Why he was acting like a jerk all of a sudden was beyond me. Ezra plodded gleefully along behind us, a borrowed book tucked under his arm.

"I think I know what they, or rather, what I was up to," Silverstein said pulling me into the elevator.

"This warranted dragging me around? Were you figuring out a way to bore the world to death?"

"No, something far worse. And, far more cunning I'm afraid," Silverstein whispered, lines of worry creasing his usually placid face.

The elevator doors closed with barely a whisper. Silverstein poked a button and we shot quickly down to the ground floor. Stepping out into the lobby I dug my heels in and gave Silverstein's arm a sharp tug.

"Are we just leaving the RV? I like the RV. We should ride in the RV," I protested, not particularly keen on walking through uptown.

"Yes, we're leaving it," he replied sadly, tossing his newly procured mobile into a trashcan.

Rounding a corner, we walked quickly through the bank lobby being careful to keep our faces turned away from the cameras. Once we set foot out into the street, it was as though I could feel the eyes of every well-to-do person looking at me, sensing my moneylessness. I wanted to go home so badly.

We followed Silverstein into a park where children played under the watchful eye of overpaid nannies beneath well-kept trees, and playground equipment covered in glossy bright paint. We walked briskly to the restrooms and piled into the men's room, turning the deadbolt behind us.

"Notice anything about the buildings in uptown?" Silverstein asked breathlessly.

"Um, they are all full of people with money?" I ventured, totally not understanding Silverstein's panic.

"They're safe. Reinforced like bunkers in case of terrorist attack, controlled and monitored by a network of computers," Silverstein began.

Ezra and I both nodded numbly in response.

"If the companies that owned them went bankrupt, they'd shut down, everyone inside being compelled to leave. Effectively evicted. Most people will wander out thinking it's a drill or exercise of some kind," Silverstein said running his fingers through his hair.

"So, a few companies are going bankrupt?"

"No, all of them will. The bank we walked out of has been using an investment strategy I must have concocted. It's been quietly investing funds into an array of investments, each designed to mature and payout to each unique primary investor."

"Who's the primary investor?"

"The bank, and everyone that has put money into it, borrowed money from it, knowingly or otherwise."

"When do the funds and investments mature?"

"In like a million years."

"I don't understand."

Silverstein nodded holding up his hand, trying to conjure a way to explain what must have been pretty complicated financial stuff to Ezra and me.

"There's only so much money in the world. What would happen if enough of it was tied up in an investment that wasn't set to payout or mature in the near future?"

"People would have to go into debt to pay their debt's debt? I don't know."

"You're closer than you think. The bank that Vance Uroboros has been quietly funneling the world's real money into has these sorts of investments, which act as cash traps. The money can't escape, so most of the largest banks have been trading and speculating on each other's debt. All the while, everyone's doctoring their financials to hide the fact that they have no real operating capital," Silverstein explained, leaning against the sink.

"Wait, aren't you Vance Uroboros? Can't you stop it?" I said slugging him.

"I don't know. I don't know."

"What happens if someone discovered the false financials?"

"All it would take is someone submitting some corporate code to one of the many Central AI terminals. It would reveal what had previously been hidden by loopholes in corporate and governmental code for decades. This has been going on for a long time I think."

"What would happen?"

"Industry and government across the world would be shut down by the Central AI when it was revealed there wasn't enough operating capital. I think only the Moon Resort and the Mars Penal Colony would be financially detached enough to escape being shut down."

"People would be forced out of their workplaces and homes in uptown zones across the world," I whispered, finally beginning to understand.

"Yes, and lacking even the possibility of acquiring the proper operating capital, none of those institutions would be allowed to reopen."

"The displaced people would filter into the downtown zones and underground looking for food and shelter while all the goods that trickle down would stop?"

Silverstein nodded solemnly.

"Why are we in the bathroom?" Ezra said, looking around disdainfully.

"This is where I do my best thinking," Silverstein said with a wink.

"Can we stop it?" I said shaking my head as I unlocked and opened the door to step outside.

"Depends. If I set the whole thing up, I know I wouldn't leave anything to chance. I'd make sure nothing got in the way of my masterstroke," Silverstein muttered.

"What if you aren't responsible? Maybe you've been working to try and stop it?" I looked to Ezra for support.

"It's possible, but unlikely given what little I've been able to see so far."

We walked quietly out of the park, and down to the tubes to use the light rail, hopefully to go home. It would be long ride to take the subway all the way downtown, and I was glad I packed a lunch. By the time we got to the platform, it was late and the regular commuters had gone home.

It wasn't long before a train came and we boarded, finding a comfy bench to sit on. Silverstein was particularly sullen, and little of the goofing off Ezra and I engaged in seemed to cheer him up. Must be rough thinking you're the one who ruined the world, and you might never remember why you were doing it in the first place.

I had a hard time believing Silverstein had set out intentionally to bring about a financial cataclysm. I wanted to believe he was a hapless pawn in all of this, or that he'd done it under duress. I wanted to believe that Silverstein was one of the good guys.

"Taylor, I want you to do something for me," Silverstein said at last, our stop rapidly approaching.

"What's that?" I replied, again at the losing end of a thumb war with Ezra.

"I want you to take Ezra back to your apartment. I want you to tell Russ what's going on and help him get the building ready to repel invaders, so to speak," Silverstein whispered reluctantly.

"What are you going to do? What if Russ isn't really our friend?"

"I'm going to try to find the code I wrote to be given to the Central AI. It wasn't at the bank building. It might be on that computer at the mansion. If Russ isn't really our friend, Ezra will know what to do."

"We should go with you," Ezra insisted.

"No!" Silverstein growled.

Ezra and I jumped in our seats. We'd never really heard Silverstein raise his voice.

"No. Please, go back to the apartment and stay there," Silverstein gently replied. "I'll join you there in a day or two. I might have made this mess, but I'd like to see if I can clean it up."

Ezra and I watched Silverstein disappear with the train as it headed back around towards uptown. I couldn't help it. I started to cry big gooey tears even though I tried like hell not to.

"He yelled at us," Ezra said frowning sadly.

"Yeah."

"We'll tie him down and tickle him until he pees when he gets back," Ezra whispered, patting me reassuringly.

I laughed a little bit and shook my head.

"I'll miss him," I said sobbing. "Even if he is a big wuss, I always feel better with him around."

"Yeah, I'll miss him, too. Even among my own people... I'm a freak. He always treats me decently," Ezra replied sadly.

"Really?"

That's when Ezra gave me the most awkward hug ever and we headed for home, down into the dark labyrinth that was downtown Port Montaigne.

CHAPTER 8

Downtown Port Montaigne, Transit Station

3:16 PM, December 23rd, 2199

Taylor's Diary, Part 3

At the time, my life was not unlike the walls in my apartment. If you were to peel back the paint, you'd find Mrs. Carbo's creepy cartoon cat wallpaper. Like so many things, I know I should have taken that wallpaper down, because even with a fresh coat of paint, deep down, I know it's still there.

The transit station was nearly empty when we arrived back in our own dark little part of Port Montaigne. Ezra and I made our way out of the station and into the streets of downtown, a perpetual paranoia echoing in our footsteps. Without the rain and the clamor of the transient population, it was literally all we could hear. Every time I took a step, I worried who might be able to hear us.

The streets, like the transit station, were conspicuously empty for a time that usually saw a lot of traffic. I had become so used to the crush of people, noise, and motion that a still and empty street was always a component of my nightmares. I kept hoping it was all a dream.

Usually the arched supports rising far above us would flicker with barrel fires, and we could hear music and the noise people made coming and going. Even the gentle breeze blowing in from the ocean did little to soothe my nerves. Something had happened while we were away in uptown.

It was near the edge of the peddlers' district when Ezra stooped down and fished up a single shell casing.

"It was recently fired. The ground shows signs of being swept, and wreaks of cleansing chemicals," Ezra reported.

Something had happened here, and someone went to great lengths to cover it up. It all ceased to surprise me anymore.

The few people who had lingered about in the aftermath told us it was the Collectors. It wasn't enough to just take what little money people could manage to make down here. They started taking people, too. I couldn't imagine why, but given the compulsory nature of downtown's police protection, it didn't bode well.

We took three full trips around the apartment building to make sure we weren't being followed or watched. Once Ezra was sure it was safe to go in, we crept in through a small window. I wanted to tell Russ we were back, but Ezra was worried about exposing ourselves or using my mobile until we'd gotten some rest and a bite to eat.

A cold can of beans and a lukewarm cup of instant coffee later, I felt better. I wished Silverstein had been there. Not to say Ezra wasn't good company, but I worried about Silverstein. He wasn't himself when we parted ways, his usual calm seem shattered by what we'd seen uptown.

I sat for an hour in my bed and scrolled through the news articles on my mobile. There was no mention of an incident in downtown, not like the established news outlets ever covered what went on in the city's underbelly. I stared at my empty email box, quietly hoping Silverstein would send me a message from wherever he was.

After a while I gave up and shut my mobile off to charge. I grabbed up a blanket and looked out into my tiny living room. Ezra was kneeling on the radiator gazing out the window.

"Worried we were followed?"

"No, I just like looking around at the outside," Ezra said putting his elbows up on the window sill.

"I would think most Drones would be made nervous by wide open spaces," I said yawning.

"Most are, a fixture of my people I suppose. For some reason, I don't have that same apprehension about it. There are others like me who quietly enjoy the wide open surface world."

"Others?"

"Type One Drones, like me. I think we were designed to have very little fear of, well... anything, I guess."

"Good night, Ezra."

Ezra stood vigil through the later part of the day and first part of the night. I had to get up and head into work for a little while. I left after being reasonably sure Ezra was comfortable. I looked around for Russ before I left, but had to settle for leaving him a note.

Getting closer to the Strip and Waffle, it was clear the streets were back to business as usual. The peddlers, dealers, and pimps were all on parade, and I was back to wishing Silverstein was walking with me. I slipped through the service entrance and walked through the storage room to the kitchen.

I went to pop in and say hello to Joe, but it looked like he had visitors in his office. The dancers breathed a sigh of relief when they saw me, and for a moment it looked like some of them wanted to talk. It struck me as odd at the time, but I just wanted to get to work, take my mind off things.

I filled the basin with water to let some pans soak, then wandered about the mostly empty club bussing tables. I pulled a few decent tips, then wandered back to my corner of the kitchen. I had just finished putting the last of the dishes in the basin to soak for a moment when I heard a commotion in the back room. I just thought it was the dancers scuffling over a feather boa or something.

I had grabbed my second dish when a hand grabbed me by the shoulder. I whirled around and saw Joe standing off to one side, a pair of rubber coat wearing goons standing in front of me. A kid dressed in a sharp uptown suit stepped in between them. He couldn't have been more than fourteen, and he was eerily familiar.

"Hello, Taylor," the kid said, extending his hand to me.

"What do they want, Joe?" I growled looking angrily over at my boss.

"Whatever it is, just give it to them," Joe said trying to calm me down.

I turned and looked intently at the kid. He had long hair stretching down past his shoulders. When he brushed it aside, that's when I recognized him. It was Silverstein, or what he probably looked like as a pimple-squeezing teenager.

"I don't have anything for you," I said. I tightened the grip on the plate still lingering in my hand.

"You miss him when he's away, don't you? He probably feels like a big brother, an easy friend, or something more than a convenient lover? You probably never trusted anyone so quickly, am I right?" the kid asked and smiled.

It was the same million dollar smile Silverstein would give me when I'd surprise him, or make him coffee, or make him socks. At least I was pretty sure about the socks. The kid wasn't wrong, I couldn't trust anyone in downtown, and I had Silverstein home with me after only knowing him a less than a day.

"I can tell by the look on your face that you're confused by all this. You needn't bother yourself with the details, but may I hazard a guess?" the kid said gesturing for his goons to back off.

"Hey, Joe's still paying me for this. Talk all you want," I said equipping my toughest expression.

"Your man, Silverstein? Whatever he's calling himself these days... he's gone off and left you to look for some sort of computer code?"

Worthless. How did this Silverstein Junior know what we were doing or why? I was more concerned with why he was talking to me about it.

"I have to laugh, your man had the code all along and never had a clue. Not his fault, but still funny," the kid said unbuttoning his suit jacket.

"If I don't come home soon, my roommate is going to come looking for me. You won't like him."

The kid laughed.

"You mean the drone holed up at your place? My team should already be done with him."

I swung the plate as hard as I could, shattering it over the kid's head. He went down hard. I knew I wouldn't get by the goons, so I wasted what little time I'd bought myself giving the kid a good kicking. Made me a feel a little better, up until one of the Collectors hit me with a stun gun.

The strange thing was, I didn't drop. I was stunned that whatever he hit me with hadn't stunned me. I know, right?

"Idiots! That won't work on her," the kid screamed, spitting out a tooth.

Joe grabbed me round the arms and held me tight while they pulled a zip tie around my wrists.

"Taylor, quit fighting them," Joe said slipping something heavy into my jacket.

I looked into Joe's eyes, he was terrified. The kid stood up, picking chunks of broken plate out of his face. He smiled, somewhat toothlessly as a result of the thrashing I'd given him.

"Take her outside. Let's get this over with," the kid said with a chuckle.

They dragged me past the dressing room where a couple of goons were holding guns on the girls. No wonder Joe was playing along. Didn't mean I had to do the same once I got outside.

They dragged me into the back of one of their black transports and held me down on the floor. A man dressed in white kneeled over me. He handed the kid a syringe filled with a slightly luminescent blue fluid. I struggled.

"Vance, you don't know what this will do exactly. She's an extremely valuable piece of hardware. It's not every day we can lay hands on something from the Lunar--"

"Shut up. After the kicking she gave me, all I need to know is that this will scramble her but good," Vance bellowed, pointing a finger at the man dressed in white.

"This might make her unusable to our rogue asset, but she might well be useless to us as well. Stop and think about what you're doing."

The kid didn't listen. He plunged the syringe into my arm and depressed the stopper. The doctor let go of my arm to try to stop him. In the struggle I reached into my jacket and grasped at the thing Joe had stuck there. Still bound, I clumsily withdrew it and pointed it at the kid pulling the trigger.

Goons pressed into me clumsily wrestling the gun away from me, blood spraying across the man in white. The lights in the transport flickered suddenly and everything went dark. There were sudden bursts of gunfire, briefly illuminating the compartment. Hot shell casings rained down around me as the goons began firing wildly inside the transport.

I rolled out the back and landed roughly on the street. I had never felt so sick in my life, like my mind was being pushed into a tight place it couldn't possibly fit. My guts churned, forcing me to lose my pancakes all over the ground. I was suddenly ice cold, but I was too weak to shiver.

I grabbed the syringe, pulled it out of my arm, and stuck it in my pocket. Already beginning to feel a little better, I tried to stand. The air got impossibly tight around me, and everything was moving so slowly. Digital readers and screens inside nearby shop windows flickered slowly, black lines dodging across images they displayed. I could see the light passing slowly through the air, motes and particles of gunpowder from the guns being fired above me, and yet I couldn't hear anything.

I looked up and could see Ezra leaping between the goons, his clawed hands grasping at their necks and wrists. He was hurt, and I could see bullets passing through the air in his direction. I leapt up and grabbed him, feeling my body press against something extremely dense.

Ezra yelped as I grabbed him. It was like he was stuck in the air by some unseen force, so I pulled hard. The world felt all wrong around me, as though everything was quickly becoming solid and immovable.

It was like running through molasses, but as slowly as I could feel myself moving, the goons were much slower. I ducked under their slow moving bullets and grasping hands easily, dragging Ezra as best as I could. My shoes disintegrated and my feet burned as every bracelet and necklace I was wearing was left behind, torn off of me by some unseen force.

I blinked.

We were blocks away now. I couldn't figure out what had happened until I checked out Ezra. He was clutching at a bullet wound in his side.

"What happened?" I asked.

I lifted his rubber suit aside to press a torn bit of my own shirt on the wound.

"You moved, so fast, blood pooled, can't see anything," Ezra said grasping about helplessly.

"I moved fast? It felt like I was running in slow motion."

"Maybe compared to everyone else, but you almost tore me in half running that fast," Ezra said wheezing.

"Oh my God! I'm so sorry, Ezra!"

This couldn't be real. What did that little creep inject me with? I had to get Ezra to a doctor, maybe someone who could help me find an antidote for whatever Silverstein Junior did to me.

I helped Ezra up, and together we limped toward Dr. Helmet's clinic. It was pretty far, and we had to squat in the shadow of more than a few abandoned buildings to avoid Collector Transports zig-zagging overhead. The last little bit was scary though, as Ezra kept nodding off on me.

We got to the clinic as the first rays of the sun were coming across the ocean, filtering past the buildings and concrete supports. Together, Ezra and I huddled in the doorway waiting for Dr. Helmet to arrive. It was a scary hour or so, but eventually he came.

"My friend needs help," I pleaded.

Dr. Helmet gave me a tight lipped glance as he looked down at Ezra. He seemed so small as the good doctor cradled him in his arms taking him inside. I watched helplessly as the doctor stitched up both the entrance and exit wounds. He gave Ezra a shot of something and shook his head.

"Drones have a physiology that is not dissimilar from humans, buy he will heal up more quickly. These antibiotics will help," Dr. Helmet said pulling a badly beaten blanket over Ezra.

"Thanks for helping him. How do you know so much about Drones?"

"He's got a lot of blood on him... most of it isn't his. Am I going to regret helping him?"

"No, he was saving me from Collectors and got shot. He's one of the good guys, really."

"What did the Collectors want with you, young lady?"

"They injected me with this," I replied producing the syringe.

Dr. Helmet took the syringe from me and used his handheld to scan it. He gazed intently at the readings, a look of confusion crossing his face. He took a sample of my blood (ouch!) and had me follow him back into his small laboratory.

"What was in the syringe?"

"My equipment is old, but I believe it to be a special catalyst designed to activate nano-technological devices and machines."

"Nano-technowhatsits?"

"Very small machines. This catalyst should be totally harmless to humans, unless they had nano... um, those very small machines lying dormant inside them."

I breathed a sigh of relief at first, until I remembered the odd side effects. I sat down in a rickety folding chair by the wall and tried to remember what happened more clearly. It was all a blur, literally.

"What did it do to me?" I asked, terrified of the answer.

"I've looked at your blood under the microscope. I must say, you are extremely interesting. Amazing even," Dr. Helmet remarked as he polished his glasses.

"Thanks, but this is the part where you tell me what it did to me," I said impatiently.

Dr. Helmet paused pulling a chair to sit in across from me. Clasping his hands in front of him, he took a deep breath, like he was about to tell me I had cancer.

"You don't have the nano machines I spoke of residing in your body--"

"That's a good thing!"

"The whole of your body is made of them. You're completely artificial, at least relative to a regular person."

"I'm a robot made of smaller robots?"

"Well, yes, after a fashion, but that description falls woefully short of describing how dizzyingly complex you are."

"Oh, okay."

Dr. Helmet suddenly conjured an expression of deep fatherly concern.

"I was under the impression you might be completely clueless about your condition. All things considered, you're taking it extremely well. In truth you're lucky I have older medical equipment that's off the grid. Newer scanning technology has probably been coded to throw false information in the event a terrestrial intelligent agent comes in for a checkup," Dr. Helmet remarked blinking his eyes in disbelief.

"Terrestrial what? Who did this to me? Why did they do it to me?" I muttered, trying to reason through what was happening.

"My dear, you don't understand. This wasn't something someone did to you. You were born, or created this way. Someone made and programmed you. I'm no expert, but you are likely one of the most ingenious intelligent agents ever created," Dr. Helmet answered, almost giddy.

I didn't have time for this. Standing up, I turned and headed for the door and almost bit my tongue in surprise. Ezra was standing in the doorway, rubbing his side.

"Ezra! You're okay!" I said hugging him.

"I heal quickly."

Dr. Helmet stood grabbing the blood sample and the syringe from the lap table. He beckoned for us to follow him, taking us into the basement. Ezra and I watched as he put both the blood sample and the syringe into the incinerator.

"You both won't be safe here for long," Dr. Helmet said walking to some boxes in the corner of the basement. "The Collectors likely have some inkling they hurt your drone friend there, and they'll be searching the clinics.

"You have a back way out?" I asked.

"No, but I've a place we can lie low for a while."

He moved a few of the boxes to the side revealing a metal grating leading down to the tunnels below. Unlocking several pad locks, he lifted the grating and began climbing down.

"Coming?" Dr. Helmet asked and disappeared down the access.

Ezra gave my arm a squeeze and turned me around to face him.

"We'll find Silverstein, I promise."

"Really?"

"I found you, didn't I?" Ezra said pulling his goggles back down over his eyes.

"I suppose you did," I said smiling at Ezra.

We climbed down into the passage and followed Dr. Helmet underground for several blocks. These weren't the lower shafts, but the drainage tunnels designed to carry flood waters back out to the sea. Ezra crept along beside me looking about nervously.

"What? What's wrong?"

"These tunnels have no trail markers."

"Markers?"

"Signs that Drones have passed through here. These tunnels have been segregated from the underground grid," Ezra said speaking loudly enough the doctor could hear.

"True," Dr. Helmet remarked without slowing.

"You had someone hack the central AI to turn the cisterns and lids underground so this place would be cut off," Ezra mused, giving me a brief look of concern.

"Well, not exactly," Dr. Helmet said, stopping next to a moss covered wall. "That explanation works well enough for my purposes though,"

He wiped the moss aside revealing what looked like a pair of blast doors. Lifting the cover on a keypad, he deftly entered a code causing the doors to slide slowly open. Ezra didn't budge.

"No offense, Doc, I'm grateful for you patching me up but--"

"What's your name?" Dr. Helmet interrupted.

"Ezra One."

"You're wise to be distrustful, but I genuinely mean you no harm," he remarked. "If anything, you're the reason I'm down here, after a fashion."

"I don't follow. Explain yourself," Ezra said pivoting around in front of me defensively.

"I'm a geneticist by trade. I lost my license to practice medicine in uptown after I absconded with key data. Various governmental agencies wanted to activate the whole of the Type One Drone population for their own uses," Dr. Helmet began.

"You worked the MDC Project?" Ezra hissed, still suspicious.

"Heaven help me, yes."

"Then you'll tell me why we were created in the first place," he said menacingly, his claws clicking neatly into place.

"That's a story best told inside, where there is a heater, a marvelous contrivance which will provide us tea, and a toaster oven. You both look like a nap would do you some good, too," Dr. Helmet said, gesturing toward the open blast doors.

We stepped inside and sat down in a narrow room. It had a single dilapidated recliner, and a battered vinyl couch. Dr. Helmet fired up a hot plate and put a kettle of water on. After we had tea, Ezra and I caught a couple hours of sleep.

I knew why Ezra was tired, he'd been shot and beaten halfway to a pulp the night before. However, I couldn't understand why I was so tired, it hadn't even been eight hours since I slept. It had to be whatever that brat injected me with.

We awoke to toast and more tea as Dr. Helmet sat in the recliner across from us and began to tell an amazing story.

"There was a war in space, just beyond the threshold of our own solar system. We were being invaded. At least, that's what we were led to believe."

"Invaded by what exactly? What is the MDC Project you and Ezra were going on about before?" I interrupted before sipping my tea.

"Information relative to the invasion was classified, my team was never briefed. What they knew for sure was that we needed shock troops, workers, doctors, and other professionals who could operate in space, aboard vessels, and in hostile environments... better than humans. *The Metasapient, Drone, and Clone Project* was supposed to be the answer."

"The MDC Project was designed to create slaves to do what humans didn't have the stomach to do themselves," Ezra muttered angrily.

"Interesting perspective, but appropriate I guess considering the outcome. The factories and processes behind the MDC were never made legal or public. Once the perceived threat was over, the Central Global Government decided to usurp control of the facilities that created and trained Metasapient creatures for their own purposes."

"What about the Drones?" I asked, looking over at Ezra.

"We designed them to survive, even if humanity did not. They were to be a last line of defense. They would be left behind in the event the invaders made their way to Earth, and wiped out humanity."

"They justified creating us to fend off an invasion? What a bunch of crap," Ezra whispered, taking his goggles off.

"Indeed?" Dr. Helmet said calmly.

I didn't understand what he was suggesting at first. Ezra's eyes turned into slits and I thought maybe he was really angry. Then the tears started to flow, he was so sad.

"I don't understand," I said trying to comfort Ezra.

"I agree, the invasion was likely a cover, and the real reasons for Drones being deployed are somewhat more sinister," Doctor Helmet stated trying to be as delicate as possible. "It is possible the Central Global Government concocted the invasion as a way to sidestep laws regulating cloning and genetic manipulation to build a slave race."

"Who would believe such a thing?" Ezra hissed.

I struggled with the concept, never having thought much beyond the small events of my own life. I lingered for a moment on those thoughts. I grew up downtown with no parents, living where I could, no one to guide me. Never even suspected I was a nano-thing-a-ma-jig.

"Please understand, I only know what I was told and had a very cursory role in the MDC Project. I know far more about the part of the project that gave birth to the Drones," Dr. Helmet began slowly.

"Type One Drones, we were made to be killers, yes?" Ezra growled angrily.

"No, of course not."

"I heard you talking upstairs, about how you might come to regret helping me. Something about most of the blood on me not being my own," Ezra snapped, waving his claw dismissively.

"Understand that some of every sample of the Metasapient, Drone, and Clone Project went rogue. I couldn't be sure you weren't one of the rogues," Dr. Helmet explained.

"I seem pretty good at destroying other people," Ezra hissed remorsefully.

"True, but you've likely only killed to protect your tribe or your friends. Have you ever killed in cold blood, because you like it? Do you not feel remorse?"

"Humans rarely seem to draw such a distinction."

"True. I believe there is a fine line between someone who is just a killer, and someone who is a protector. Ezra, I think you're a protector. It is what we designed the Type One Drones to do, preserve the lives of the others." Dr. Helmet put his hand on Ezra's shoulder.

"I have met few humans half as noble as the least altruistic Drone," Ezra muttered batting Dr. Helmet's hand away.

"I wish I had something more to tell you. Most of the members of my team have passed away or vanished. I still have the data I took with me when I quit the project," Dr. Helmet remarked sadly.

"No. I've heard enough. Let's get out of here, Taylor," Ezra said tugging on my arm.

"Thanks for the tea!" I said. I followed Ezra out through the blast doors.

Dr. Helmet stepped out into the tunnel behind us shutting the blast doors. He escorted us back out through the clinic once he was sure it was safe. He caught Ezra by the shoulder as we were leaving and gave him some extra bandages.

"Thanks," Ezra said tucking them away.

"If you change your mind about that data, you know where to find me."

Ezra and I made our way back downtown just as a black transport carrying a bunch of Collectors landed nearby. From hiding, we watched them question Dr. Helmet fruitlessly. Eventually they got back in their Spookymobile and took off, leaving the doctor to open the clinic for the day.

Ezra and I crouched inside a cardboard box behind a dumpster for the majority of the morning planning our next move. We had no idea where Silverstein had gone, and trying to travel in uptown during the day was a sure way to attract attention. We decided the best thing to do was spend the day following the Collectors and try to find out from where they were operating.

"What do you think really happened to Silverstein? How he came to be in that alley unconscious and without a memory," I asked following Ezra through an alley.

"It is not what either of you suspect, that much I'm certain of," Ezra replied.

"How do you know?"

"My nose knows. Silverstein, his murderous double, the mansion, his office at Uroboros Financial... none of it smells right when compared to one another," Ezra remarked, after taking a moment to find the right words.

"I think I understand what you're saying."

We walked along the street beneath the tattered awning of the old glitz and nightclub row, trying to watch what few of the Collector's transports we could. It seemed like they were taking off and landing near the waterfront, a place I was loathe to visit. It was full of establishments designed to cater to men who had been at sea for months, warehouses, and huge cranes used to offload ships.

All our observations from the ground kept pointing to somewhere in that area. It was a long walk, and this was a part of downtown Ezra and I were unfamiliar with. It was almost nightfall before we found what we were looking for.

The sign on the chain link fence around the property read "Alphadein Inc. No Trespassing." Ezra pressed up against the fence, and we both gazed about to the dark interior of the lot. There were lots of those same black transports, wheeled trucks, and a large concrete industrial structure.

"Ezra, now that we've found where they hang out, what do we do?"

"Watch."

That's exactly what we did, all night. Thankfully the Collectors weren't good at maintaining the property so there were plenty of bushes and trash heaps outside giving us places to hide. We watched as the transports would land, sometimes unloading what looked like small sacks of something heavy. Other times, they'd unload a person, gagged, bound, and blindfolded.

"Extortion, kidnapping, and they tried to murder me. I'm really beginning to dislike these guys," Ezra whispered.

"What are we going to do about it?"

"I'd like to find out how they're connected to Silverstein. More than that, I'd like to know if Silverstein is a clone of this Vance Uroboros character, or the original article."

"Did you kill the young Vance Uroboros that injected me with that stuff?"

"I think so, but it all went down so fast."

I toyed with my hair nervously. It seemed like none of us were who we appeared to be. I hoped Silverstein wasn't mixed up in all this so deep we couldn't get him out.

"What about me? Dr. Helmet thinks I'm a robot," I muttered still toying with my hair.

"We'll get a second opinion. You don't look or feel like any robot I've ever seen," Ezra whispered as he smiled.

"Thanks, that means a lot coming from you," I said hugging Ezra.

"It does?" he replied, eyes wide.

"You're my friend. You came to my rescue when they tried to truss me up and bring me to this place we've been watching. Of course what you say means something," I said slugging Ezra playfully.

"Oh."

CHAPTER 9

November 4th, 2127 - 72 years previous to shutdown.

"I haven't been back to Earth since I left the Factory. Do you think we'll get to do anything fun while we're there?" Athos One asked, loading .308 rifle rounds into a long clip.

The transport shook violently for a few moments making all the Drones insides grab their restraints tightly.

"We've been sitting at the rim just past Mars for three and ten, all I want is a candy bar, preferably something with peanuts and a piece of real fruit," Ezra One said, checking his communications equipment.

"When I can get it, I've been listening to the BBC almost every night. There have been armed revolts in a dozen major cities. Even credit says we're dropping into an urban theater," Calvin One grumbled.

The indicator light on the wall above where Athos One was sitting turned from green to yellow and a countdown appeared. The Drones all looked up, each knowing they were only minutes from Earth now. They'd put down violent labor revolts on Mars among the prison populations, and knew how tricky urban warfare could be. None of them was looking forward to the prospect of having to do it again.

"Tell me again why we do this?" Athos One asked.

"Because we are tailored lifeforms and we'll all get sent back to the Factory for 'reprogramming' if we don't?" Calvin One growled.

"No, because no human has what it takes to do what we Drones do," Ezra One said, holding his tiny hand up for a high five.

He wasn't left hanging. They all took great pride in what they did and knew that they often did things that humanity couldn't because of their unique physiology and resistance to stress. In spite of Calvin One being a perpetual rain cloud about the whole thing, this would be one more chance to help humanity and keep innocent people safe.

"Was there anything on the BBC about these armed revolts? How are they armed exactly, and what sort of tactics do they employ?" Ezra One asked.

"No, and you'd think we would have gotten better intel before being dropped in. It's all been pretty last minute and haphazard. Didn't even get the standard on-screen briefing or anything," Athos One replied.

"I'm just glad we have one pygmy among us. Most of the other teams don't have a scout," Calvin One said, gesturing to Ezra One.

"Hey, did Calvin just look for a silver lining? Those therapy tapes from the Factory must be working at last?" Athos One joked.

"He might be more cheerful if you'd quit picking on him," Ezra One said, performing a final weapons check.

"Yeah, but what fun would that be?" Athos One laughed.

Ezra put his hand up to cover his earbud and listened intently.

"Make sure your cowls are up and you've got your long coats on. We'll be making a night drop and moving to intercept the armed insurgents. We are clear to kill and green-lit for lethal ammunition, this sounds pretty serious," Ezra One said, turning to the rest of the squad.

"Chelsea Six, you getting any sort of feeling from the ground?" Athos One said, turning to the squad's psychic.

"We're still in Earth's atmosphere, but I do have a bad feeling about this whole thing," Chelsea Six replied, holding her hands up to her temples.

"Suggested course of action?" Ezra One asked, unhooking his restraints.

"We should kill the relay on board our drop vessel," Chelsea Six replied hesitantly.

The Drones in the squad froze knowing what that likely meant. The Central Global Government was going to disavow whatever they were about to do and would likely use the relay to shut their weapons down. It would make it easier for them to be rounded up and sent back to the Factory in the aftermath.

"I'll do it," Calvin One said, unhooking his restraints.

"You sure?" Ezra One whispered, putting his tiny hand on Calvin One's arm.

"Yeah," Calvin One replied. He hit the button to open the airlock separating the squad row from the rest of the ship.

The ship was completely empty, kept in the air by a sophisticated autopilot. Calvin One took off his boots before continuing down the corridor to where the ship's onboard systems were mounted off to one side. He took a deep breath, reached over and put his powerfully clawed hand on the ship's relay system that governed communications to the squad, their tactical harnesses, and weapons.

"Unauthorized personnel accessing systems, deploying countermeasures," an automated voice sounded over the transport's intercom.

The relay made a crackling plastic sound and the stink of burning circuits as Calvin One crushed it with his hand. The indicator lights on his tactical harness went from green to red as it flooded his body with a powerful toxin that paralyzed him. He fell to the floor feeling the toxin work its way to his lungs and organs.

Ezra One did his best to comfort Chelsea Six, but she could empathically feel every sensation that Calvin One felt as he died. The rest of the Drones in the squad just lowered their heads and looked down at their own tactical harnesses. The indicator lights flickered and went dark in time with Calvin One's eyes.

"Harnesses off," Ezra ordered, gritting his teeth.

The squad took their tactical harnesses off putting their gear into pockets or tucked inside their ballistic vests. Ezra went out and got Calvin One's body and dragged it back into the squad hold and strapped him in where he belonged. Suddenly, Ezra's earbud squawked to life.

"Drone Team 045, report, your relay just went dead," said the automated system voice.

"We are green, onboard malfunction. We are still clear to deploy," Ezra One replied.

"Acknowledged, clear to deploy," the automated system voice replied.

Ezra strapped himself back in as the turbulence began to get worse. The rest of the squad looked suitably morose at the loss of Calvin One. As much as he'd been teased, he was the only one besides Ezra willing to make that sacrifice. Athos One was particularly downcast, humbled by his teammate's action.

"We can feel bad later. Right now we've got a job to do. Let's get down there, do what we came to do and try to avoid getting recycled," Ezra One barked.

The transport leveled out coming in smooth. There were no portholes and no way of knowing where they were. As the cabin began to depressurize, they could smell the ocean and the smog of a big city. They were on Earth now.

The whole vehicle began to slow while losing altitude. It seemed to take forever, but eventually they could feel the telltale shift as the transport began making a silent decent. The hatch at the rear of the squad hold opened and the Drones began pouring out onto a rooftop, each giving Calvin One a gentle pat or squeeze as they went by.

Ezra One dropped out last, his larger teammates gathering around as he pulled out his GPS enabled data slate and waited for intel. The tiny screen lit up with contact all along the streets to the north. They were in uptown, Port Montaigne in the United States. It was the last country Ezra One had anticipated having to confront armed insurgents.

"Drone 045 requesting identity of insurgent force," Ezra said, holding his hand up over his earbud.

"Political dissidents unhappy with recent Global Labor Act. Central Global Government Trade Commission Building is their target," the automated voice replied.

Ezra motioned for his fellow Drones to follow him as he kicked in the roof access to the building. They sprinted down through the building to the access stairs and made their way to the street. They dimmed the indicators on their weapons and circled around to an alley adjoining the street. All they could see was what appeared to be a crowd of unarmed youths carrying signs, banging drums, and chanting.

"Drone 045, negative contact. We've got civic uprising. There is no armed insurgency as indicated by GPS data, please advise," Ezra One said, motioning for his squad to lower their weapons.

"Ezra One, this is Captain Jameson. We are running a joint COIN operation with the CGG to disperse these youths, you are clear to fire," a voice said coming over the radio.

Ezra glanced down at his data slate, the captain's authorization codes appearing on the screen.

"Drone 045, negative," Ezra One replied. "This is unarmed civil unrest, deploy local law enforcement or U.S. National Guard. Lethal force is not warranted."

"You've got your orders," Captain Jameson replied.

Ezra shut down the audio input on his communicator and turned to look back at the rest of the squad.

"Chelsea Six, criminal motivations of the crowd. I know it's a lot of people to try and read, but what do they intend to do?" Ezra One asked.

"They are attempting to gather and protest some new law that has deprived them of fair access to employment," Chelsea Six whispered, her psychic presence suddenly filling the alleyway. "There are kids as young as fifteen out there."

"You guys good with firing on a crowd of unarmed civilians?" Ezra One asked, already knowing the answer.

"No way," Athos One said, shaking his head along with the rest of the squad.

"Yeah, this isn't Mars where a group of heavily armed convicts were trying to overthrow the Bureau of Wardens."

Ezra clicked audio input back on and shouldered his rifle.

"Captain Jameson, this is Ezra One, we do not see an armed insurgency. We've zero contact and no target, please advise." Ezra One motioned for the squad to assume a safe distance.

"I'm watching you via satellite surveillance," Captain Jameson replied. "You're in the alley right next to where the insurgents are moving. I understand they don't look dangerous, but merely containing them with the National Guard or the police won't send the right message here. These are dangerous political dissidents, and you've got orders to fire on them. Comply with the orders or die."

"With all due respect, sir, you can kiss my pale, genetically tailored ass. We aren't shooting a bunch of peaceful kids," Ezra One replied defiantly.

"We've already got CGG kill teams on site to open fire as soon as they reach the trade commission. You're throwing your lives away for nothing," Captain Jameson growled.

"Not anymore we aren't," Ezra One said, shutting his communication gear down.

The Drones in the squad looked relieved as Ezra took his headset off and put it in his rucksack.

"Uh-oh," Chelsea Six said, already knowing what Ezra One was about to do.

"There are an unknown number of CGG wetworks teams standing by at the trade commission to fire on the crowd once they've assembled. I'm going to go to try to stop them. If you go back to the transport the worst that will happen is a trip back to the Factory for reprogramming. If you go with me, you'll be running from Earth's global government the rest of your lives," Ezra said, readying his weapon and pulling his goggles on.

"I'm with you," Athos One replied grimly readying his weapon.

"Won't they just send a signal to shut our weapons down?" Chelsea Six asked.

"We're still on Martian Central spectrum and broadband, it'll take hours assuming the Martian Government even obliges them," Ezra replied. "I've already sent a transcript of my conversation with the general that should get there ahead of their request to shut us down."

The rest of the squad readied their weapons and dropped their goggles down over their eyes. They knew they would be facing elite and probably better equipped teams of humans already bent on killing anyone working against the CGG's agenda. Some of them would die, but at their core they knew they were meant to do one thing, and one thing only: protect humanity.

They would do this, even if it meant protecting humanity from itself.

Ezra pressed around the corner as fast as his short legs would carry him, the rest of the Drones plodding along silently behind him. The kill team was just ahead taking up positions on balconies and behind planters using stealth enabled armor. Chelsea Six reached out with her mind guiding each of the Drones in the squad, helping them see where each of the kill team was hiding.

"Contact!" Ezra whispered harshly, dropping to a firing position in the street just outside the alleyway.

The squad responded with controlled burst fire focusing on one to three targets at a time per Chelsea's direction. They worked like a single organism while the humans panicked and called out on their radios. They returned fire but mostly at the ghostly flickers of psychic fire Chelsea Six used to pollute their minds.

Ezra ran over to one of the fallen CGG troopers and picked up his communicator. He looked at the display. He frowned and tossed the device to the ground sniffing the trooper's clothing. Reaching into a pocket he produced a peanut bar and held it aloft like it was a trophy.

"What do we do now?" Athos One asked.

"There are four more of these teams arrayed around the Trade Commission, or on their way," Ezra said sadly, taking a bite of the peanut bar and handing it off to the nearest Drone.

"There's no way we can stop them all," Chelsea Six said sadly.

"We have to try," Athos One said, giving the fallen trooper a kick.

"For Calvin One," Ezra One said with a nod.

"For Calvin One," the other Drones replied.

They sprinted for the trade commission just as the protesters could dimly be seen ten blocks away. Chelsea Six took the lead beside Ezra to help guide them to their targets faster. The street was clear of vehicles, planters or other sorts of cover. It looked as though the CGG had made the area more ideal for killing the protestors.

"The kill teams are in fortified elevated positions," Chelsea Six said, breathlessly. "We can get to one by doing a building entry but we wouldn't be able to engage the others in time. If we engage from the street, we will be able to fire on more of them, but we'll probably be cut down in the process."

"Athos One, take four of us and Chelsea to the building on the west side and perform a tactical entry," Ezra One said, pointing to four of the best in the squad to follow Athos. "I will take the rest of the squad into the street and try and keep them busy while focusing our fire on the north and east."

"No, I'll lead the street team. You're better at close quarters fighting than I am and I've got better eyes," Athos One said, stepping toward the street.

"You'll be killed," Chelsea Six said, raising her goggles so she could wipe tears from her eyes.

"There are two thousand people, mostly kids, counting on us. This is what I was created to do, die so they wouldn't have to," Athos One replied.

Ezra One watched for a moment as his friends went and took up positions at the edge of the alleyway, then turned and motioned for the rest to follow him west.

CHAPTER 10

Downtown Port Montaigne - Alphadein Incorporated Facility

5:27 PM, December 25th, 2199

Ezra's War Journal Part 1

I'm not so good at telling stories. Nevertheless, I'll do my best to recount what happened next.

I could see them clearly as they went in and out of the transports. They were carrying Leopold Arms Eagle Class revolvers, each loaded with seven rounds of thirty-eight caliber. I'd fought the Collectors up and personal now, and suspected they had Seraphim Company combat armor under those rubber suits. My claws only seemed to reach them high on the neck or low on the wrists.

We were about to pack it in when Taylor's TI-201 mobile device beeped. She thumbed over to her mailbox on the screen and reported that Silverstein had made contact. She told me that he wanted to meet at the midtown docks near the fish market. Taylor and I talked strategy about the best way to make our way to the rally point.

"Taylor, do you even know where that is?"

"No, we'll have to wing it."

"Can't that mobile of yours pull up maps of the city?"

"For uptown, yeah."

"Wow, that is just so handy for folks like us."

"Tell me about it."

We abandoned our surveillance of the Alphadein Incorporated facility to make our way toward the rally point in midtown. It required some asking of directions, and at least one veiled threat to one of the locals. We walked approximately eight miles to reach the base of midtown, overlooking the ocean.

The Atlantic Ocean was beautiful. A few picture books and the National Geographic magazines at Dr. Helmet's office I managed to look through did not do it justice. Taylor had to pull me away, or I'd have stared at it for hours. Sometimes I think I'd have made a better surveyor than a soldier.

Midtown is a series of large concrete platforms adjoined by service elevators and staircases. People come up from downtown if they have the skill to make things while people from uptown come down to slum and look for cheap goods. It is a peaceful compromise between two distinctly different worlds filled with music, color, and fish markets.

The journey would have been quicker, but Taylor had to stop at every vendor who had anything remotely colorful. She stopped to consider scarves, inspect clay pots, and handle vintage records. I was pretty impatient to get going, until she bought me a hot dog.

I had never had one before. It was a long cylinder of questionable meat, surrounded in a bread-like substance, and topped with all manner of squeezable garnish and chopped vegetables. If Drones typically had money for such things, one could make a mint selling them in the underground to be sure.

I regretted not being able to eat the whole thing, but it wasn't anything Taylor couldn't remedy. She swallowed the remainder along with her own hot dog without missing a beat.

"I'm certain you aren't a robot."

"Why's that, Ezra?"

"You're a garbage disposal."

She slugged me.

When we arrived at the fish market, Silverstein was nowhere to be found. We found a spot in the market that was unoccupied and hopped up on the counter to sit. The market goers passed by slowly in time with my slowly waning patience.

"When did he say to meet him here?"

"As soon as we could. Want another hot dog?" Taylor replied looking about for a vendor.

"Gods no, but he needs to hurry. It'll be dark soon."

"Relax, take a deep breath, and enjoy the scenery. Sheesh."

That was the problem though. I couldn't calm down, or relax, especially not around all these people. Any one of them could be a Collector agent, someone sent to spy on us, or just your random slaver looking to put us on a ship for quick cash. I didn't understand how Taylor could so cavalier about our situation.

At least twice while we had been sitting there, the same pair of guys passed us. One was wearing coveralls and a straw hat while the other had on a pair of shorts and a colorful t-shirt. They both had all the piercings and body modification of someone from downtown, but the attitude of an uptowner.

On the third pass, they approached us. The younger of the two, the one wearing shorts, waved and smiled in greeting.

"Hey there, you interested in some work?"

Taylor didn't even look up from the game she was playing on her mobile.

"We're fine, thanks," she replied.

"Party later, want to go?" the guy in the coveralls chimed in.

"You guys are so lame, go troll for suckers somewhere else," Taylor said laughing a little bit.

They both got really angry all of a sudden. The one in the coveralls turned and looked about to make sure no one was watching while the other grabbed Taylor.

"I think you and your little brother should come with us," he growled.

I leapt up, taking a quick swipe at his arm. He reeled back in pain as I grabbed him around the shoulders, riding him all the way to the ground. His head made a thick hollow sound as it hit the concrete.

I whirled around to face the guy with the coveralls flashing him my claws. He was already running. Taylor hopped down and gave the kid wearing the shorts a kick to the ribs.

"Jerk!"

"He's crying," I observed.

"You barely scratched him, they seriously need to screen out the wusses when they recruit spotters," Taylor remarked coolly.

"Spotters?"

"For slavers, human traffickers."

"Who would want to traffic in humans? They're all pretty worthless from what I've seen," I growled, giving the spotter a kick of my own.

He writhed about, eventually regaining his composure and his footing. We watched as he ran into the crowd already gathering.

"There you are," Silverstein said, stepping up from a nearby staircase.

Taylor waved almost frantically as she leapt onto Silverstein. I was glad to see him, too. After detaching Taylor, Silverstein handed me a small object wrapped in paper. Upon opening it, I gazed inside and found a shiny new mobile, a TI-202.

"For me?"

"Yeah, I got myself one, too. Taylor already has one, so all I brought her was a hug."

"Not true, you guys have newer mobiles than I do now! No fair!" Taylor pouted.

"Didn't you tell me a while back you've lost every mobile you've owned except for your current one?" Silverstein teased.

"Phooey."

We followed Silverstein to a restaurant with a view of the ocean and ordered something called "fish and chips". I listened to Silverstein intently as I ate the salty potatoes and breaded fish. I really wasn't hungry, but I couldn't help myself.

"I went into uptown and managed to track down an honest to goodness Mechanic," Silverstein began, taking another bite of clam chowder.

"What's that?" Taylor and I asked in unison.

"They are like techno-shamans. They can feel machines, even manipulate them with their minds. They're rare in the extreme, but I needed help finding the code Uroboros Financials plans to use to exploit the accounting fraud going on worldwide," Silverstein whispered, leaning in so only we could hear.

"That's what they're called?" Taylor inquired. "Uroboros Financials? Are they the ones running the Collectors, too?"

"Worldwide, pulling as much physical cash out of the streets as they can. The whole organization has gotten incredibly corrupt though. I can't tell what they originally intended to do funneling all that money to those accounts," Silverstein remarked, shaking his head.

"What did the Mechanic say?" I asked, reaching for Silverstein's lingering potatoes.

"That the code was off-grid. He said I transferred it to a system with an almost impregnable firewall, that promptly went offline... and stayed offline ever since," Silverstein muttered sadly.

"Do you even remember doing that?"

"No."

We sat there quietly for a few moments, taking it all in as I tried in vain to eat the last of the breaded fish. Taylor looked ill for a moment, then began to relate the story of how we ran into a much younger version of Silverstein, what he said to her, the injection, Dr. Helmet, and the show stopper.

"Dr. Helmet thinks I'm some sort of robot," Taylor blurted out finally.

"Garbage disposal maybe," Silverstein quipped.

"Is this Pick-on-Taylor day? I'm serious, he said I was a robot made of millions of tiny robots," Taylor exclaimed angrily.

The rest of the Fish and Chips place went silent as people turned to look at Taylor. She smiled sheepishly then sank back into her seat. For once, I wasn't the weirdest person in the room.

"You shot me?" Silverstein asked quietly.

"Well, no, not you. A younger you who was trying to inject me with something to 'mess me up'," Taylor replied looking mightily uncomfortable.

"If it's true, and you're some sort of machine, maybe I transferred the code to you somehow?"

"I think I would remember that."

"Right, we can't both be amnesiacs. That's my shtick anyway."

Taylor sighed loudly kicking her feet under the table in consternation. None of this made sense to me either.

"Is a computer always aware of everything it receives by air or wire?" I asked.

Silverstein gave me a blank expression at first then reached across the table grabbing Taylor's mobile. She protested at first, but Silverstein shushed her.

"Taylor, you told me sometime when we first met that you've lost every mobile you've owned save this one right?"

"Well, yeah."

Silverstein clicked open the mobile and thumbed through the data on it.

"The code is on here."

"What?"

"Your mobile is set to route all data traffic through a separate server that's rebroadcasting the signal. This separate server is handling all the traffic going to or from this mobile device," Silverstein said smiling.

"Where's the separate server?" Taylor said looking around.

"Right here. It's you, Taylor. You're the one routing the signal. You're the firewall the Mechanic was talking about. It's the only explanation," Silverstein replied chuckling.

"Wow. Well, I was pretty determined not to lose this one," she said taking her mobile back.

"An act of your own will then. You couldn't lose this device because it was constantly talking to you. Subconsciously, you always know where it is," Silverstein said nodding.

"How did this happen?"

"Before I lost my memory, I knew who and what you were. I was probably downtown looking for you. Just a guess, but it's plausible."

Watching Taylor and Silverstein talk during this moment was surreal. Not being particularly good at reading humans, I wasn't sure whether they trusted each other more or less. Like all mysteries, the journey to the truth can sometimes be more rewarding than the destination.

"What do we do next? If I have the code, this is a good thing, right?" Taylor said gazing blankly at her mobile.

"We'd have to input it directly, past the firewalls around the CGG's central AI," Silverstein said shaking his head.

"Where is it?" I asked, ready to get the thing done.

"That's the problem, the main terminal for that particular intelligent agent is in Helsinki, Finland, and heavily guarded," Silverstein replied.

"So that's it, there's nothing we can do to stop this financial crap storm from shutting down most of the planet?" she whispered dejectedly.

"From what the Mechanic told me, our meddling may have pushed up the timetable. Whoever is responsible for this will put this into motion within a few days," he replied.

"Wait, are we sure the code was designed to stop this banking apocalypse? Or is it what they need to get the ball rolling? Nothing the bad guys have done recently has made that clear," I asked quietly.

"No way of knowing for sure, and there's nothing saying they don't have a backup copy, either. We need to get the code to the Mechanic I contacted and have him look at it. Maybe there's still something we can do," Silverstein said as he stood up from the table.

"Can we trust this Mechanic?" I asked.

"He didn't want to help me, and he doesn't advertise his services. It took some convincing to get him to aid me at all or even listen," Silverstein replied.

"His reluctance lends him credibility?" Taylor said, nodding slightly.

"It was the best I could do, and far better than approaching someone that seemed too eager for access to the code," Silverstein said, his tone mirroring the worry both Taylor and I shared.

We departed the restaurant and walked up several sets of stairs, going platform to platform towards uptown. When we got there, Silverstein led us to a parking structure where he had a small transport waiting. We climbed aboard without question, not certain of where he was going to take us.

We drove through uptown for hours, until we finally broke out of the city into the outside. I saw my first forest, and a deer. There are no such animals or plants underground as there are above ground. I was entranced, and the hours passed quickly as day turned to night and back to day once more.

The transport ambled up off the main road onto a dirt one, taking us back into the forest. I could see a large concrete structure rising in the distance, the better part of it overgrown with ivy and vines. We stopped at the fence that surrounded the complex and waited as the gate painfully creaked open.

The grounds around the garden were dotted with pens containing domesticated animals and plots containing gardens. Someone was living here, off the grid with their own power source. It reminded me a lot of my home, except that it was above ground.

Silverstein's transport rumbled to a halt and came to rest on the uneven ground with a crunch. Taylor threw up her hands and cheered, startling me out of my own personal haze. After a good yawn, and a stretch, I dropped out of the transport where Silverstein and Taylor were waiting.

"First one on, last one off," Silverstein quipped.

"I like the ones that fly better," I replied, placing my hand on the hull of the vehicle.

"Where are we?" Taylor asked running her hand over some planted flowers.

"I've only ever talked to Matthias online via a video feed. He's supposed to be one of the oldest and most proficient Mechanics in the world. If anyone can help me figure out what the code is for, he can," Silverstein replied, leading us up to the huge complex.

"That would have gone a long way to convincing us this was a good idea," Tayler stated impatiently.

"I dared not even speak his name within city limits."

We walked up stairs fashioned from old railroad ties similar to what I'd seen in the subway tunnels near my home. I could hear strange winged creatures chattering in the trees above us as we did. I didn't want to go inside the complex, preferring to explore the outside we were walking through. It was not meant to be.

The vault-like doors to the complex opened slowly. Once I stepped inside my suspicions were mostly confirmed. This place was a converted water tank that probably used to supply the large town nearby. Matthias had drained the water, cut holes for access and air conditioning and armored the interior to protect it and make it almost undetectable.

We walked across an expanded metal walkway through a tunnel with a rounded ceiling. The space below the walkway was full of wires, pipes, hydraulic hoses and other evidence of heavy machinery. The tunnel followed the curvature of the interior of the water tank angling down slowly, eventually meeting up with some stairs.

A commercial grade sliding door and another twenty feet of tunnel later, we found ourselves in a large underground chamber that housed what looked like several military grade vehicles and suits of powered armor. At the center were several pieces of heavy machinery and a half dozen work tables. Each table displayed a work already in progress.

"This place looks kind of like Ezra's home, before the junk sale," she said putting her hand on one of the painted steel walls.

"Ezra?" Silverstein said, turning back to look at me.

"We didn't build our underground hovels, they were designed for us by someone working the MDC Project," I replied looking around at the eerily familiar place.

Doors at the far end of the chamber opened slowly to reveal a man with shoulder length white hair and wearing a lab coat. He was taller than most humans I'd seen, with a thin nose and larger than average hands. His eyes darted up at us as he walked in then back down to the electronic slate he held in his hand.

From behind him, a small pill shaped robot appeared and came to hover at his side, its spindly mechanical arms dangling comically at its sides. Spectacles perched precariously at the end of his nose, the man reviewed something on his device. He cleared his throat before handing his slate and glasses off to the mechanical assistant floating beside him.

"Silverstein and company, I presume. Welcome to my home. My name is Matthias Ericsson and this is my assistant, Mod-Bot," the man said descending the stairs toward the work area of the lap.

"Yeah, I'm Silverstein and this is Taylor and Ezra."

Matthias and Silverstein shook hands and we all sat down around the least cluttered work table.

"You have some code you'd like me to look at?"

"Yes, Matthias. Taylor, if you wouldn't mind?"

She took out her mobile and placed it in Matthias's hands. He held the mobile in the palm of his hand then closed his eyes. The screen on the mobile lit up suddenly, its screen rapidly displaying every element of the operating system and the data stored within. It blinked madly for several seconds. Matthias took a deep breath, then gave the mobile back to Taylor.

"Before we begin, I must ask you a few questions" Matthias whispered, leaning in with both hands on the table. "I need to know what sort of people you are before I reveal anything to you."

"How do we know if we can trust you?" Taylor asked. Her cheeks grew red with anger at having her integrity questioned.

Matthias then turned his gaze to me.

"Ezra, are you a Type One?"

"Yes," I replied after some hesitation.

"Are you unsure, or ashamed?"

"Dr. Helmet already tried to tell me what I am. If you're going to do the same, this conversation is over," I replied pushing some of what was on the table to the floor with a crash.

"You've met Helmet, have you?" Matthias replied, as matter-of-fact as possible. "He designed the genetic code that would predispose Drones to the duties to which they were assigned. After many long years of work, he was allegedly fired from the MDC Project for gross incompetence."

"Can't say I'm surprised."

"Yes, it turns out he had given each Drone a powerful ethical and moral compass. It was extremely difficult for the corrupt Central Global Government to use them for police action where innocent people might be killed. Drones were so concerned with peace and protecting the weak they were of little use to an oppressive global government." Matthias stated, his gaze fixed upon me.

"I don't understand. The rival tribe that lives near mine has no problem hurting surface dwellers," I replied, almost afraid of the answer.

"The MDC project spanned decades and involved hundreds of scientists, but a handful of them were really influential. About twenty-five percent of the Drone population was manufactured after Dr. Helmet's departure. They had to be decommissioned because they were too unpredictable. Helmet and I were colleagues on the MDC Project with a man named Maurice Madmar, a brilliant cyberneticist," Matthias said, sliding an old photo across the table to me.

"I was created to protect people?" I replied, gazing at the photo of Helmet, Ericsson, and Madmar, their name tags readable on their lab coats.

"I think you are probably aware of this fact already."

"Why were most of us abandoned then? To turn wrenches in the tunnels?"

"Most of you were built for that purpose. Only a few Type One Drones were created to keep those communities safe from harm or those that would attempt to exploit them."

"Ezra's perception seems to be different from you own, Matthias," Silverstein replied.

"I should hope so. How old are you, Ezra?" Matthias said putting the photograph back in his pocket.

"Eighty-seven."

"Damn!" Taylor giggled.

I blushed uncontrollably, and even now I'm not sure why.

"One of the first. You're a pygmy variant with claws, designed specifically as a man hunter. Less than a half of one percent of all Type One Drones were made in this way. I bet you're three times faster and ten times stronger than a regular man, despite your size."

"He is, and I think he's more aware of himself than you give him credit for," Silverstein said, somewhat impatiently.

"We are definitely probing one another for truth, are we not? The infamous Vance Uroboros, enemy of the Central Global Government, manipulator, outlaw, and idealist. Not sure why you're here," Matthias replied, turning his attention to Silverstein.

"My name is Silverstein. I don't know who this Vance character is."

"You have cloned yourself so many times in a vain attempt to maintain control over your anti-government network," Matthias replied, his face turning to stone. "I wonder if a few of them have gone rogue with their own agenda."

"Look, old man--"

"Old man? You may not look it, Silverstein, or whatever you call yourself, but you're older than I am. Neat trick by the way, being able to manipulate how old or young you look. Handy in dodging the authorities," Matthias rumbled angrily.

"If Ezra is 87, that would make Doctor Helmet really old," Taylor said incredulously.

Matthias nodded slightly and picked up the old photograph. "Indeed, he and Maurice Madmar were some of the first on the project, and both are older than any normal human has right to be. They appeared to be old men when I joined the project as a young programmer."

"Are you going to help us or what?" Silverstein replied, sitting back and folding his arms.

"That depends. Where is the catalyst your organization stole?"

"Catalyst? What catalyst?" Silverstein said turning and looking back toward Taylor and me.

"Under a hunk of concrete behind my apartment in downtown Port Montaigne," Taylor replied, deep in thought.

"The chemicals, planted in the laundry cart, when we moved the guns for the Drones--" Silverstein whispered.

"We didn't know what it was we had, still don't," I said in earnest to Matthias.

Matthias's stony expression melted somewhat, comprehending that we were likely pawns in a bigger game.

"Tell me everything," Matthias said pulling a bottle and several glasses from a cabinet beneath the work table.

We began to relate the entire story. We told him whatever we could remember. When we got to the part where one of Silverstein's clones went insane and killed two people, Matthias stopped me mid-statement.

"You said the clone wasn't Silverstein? That the smell was wrong?" Matthias said thoughtfully.

"Right. Didn't smell like anything I've ever smelled before."

"Did it smell like this?" Matthias asked, sliding a plastic container over to me.

I opened the container. Inside were several biological and mechanical components suspended in a clear jelly, designed to preserve them I assumed. I sniffed the contents then slid it back over to Matthias.

"Yeah, that's what I smelled."

"A cyborg then. That wasn't one of Vance's, eh... Silverstein's clones. This is bad," Matthias said covering his face with his hands.

"Cyborgs convincing enough to pass as a person are illegal," Taylor remarked quietly.

"Madmar is the only one with the tech to make a cyborg like that. He's also the only one depraved enough to also make one into a deranged killer," Matthias whispered grimly.

"He tried to have me killed, then hijacked my... Vance's clone network? Why?" Silverstein ventured, and like me, not grasping the big picture.

"You... Vance Uroboros discovered that the Central Global Government was attempting to isolate ninety percent of the world's wealth to a handful of investments they controlled. From the intelligence I've been able to gather, Vance and the network were trying to stop it, push that wealth back out to regular people," Matthias stated plainly, sliding his data slate over to Silverstein.

"But something went wrong," Silverstein replied, looking at the data slate.

"I didn't see it until now. I thought you'd just gotten greedy, but it's clear that Madmar has been pulling the strings of your operation for at least a year now," Matthias growled, banging his hand on the table.

"What's he planning to do?" Taylor asked.

"Just what it looks like. He'll bankrupt the world. Power and services around the globe go offline. All the secure structures that house governments, the banking industry and similar will deploy countermeasures expelling everyone inside. Then, once they are clear... the buildings will go into lockdown, effectively locking humanity out of their own house," Matthias whispered angrily.

"Millions of people could die. Is there a way back into those structures, get the power back on?" I asked anxiously.

"The most important buildings worldwide have been modified to resist terrorist attacks and similar. Once they lock up, it'll be impossible to get inside without destroying them in the process," Matthias said standing up from his seat.

"Can the code stored on Taylor's mobile help?" Silverstein said.

"Yes and no. Before you lost your memory, or whatever has happened to you, you must have discovered what Taylor was. That's why you sent her the code. She's one of the few on earth with the power to protect it," Matthias said.

"Wait, I don't have any power. I was left on the streets of downtown Port Montaigne, grew up there. I've never done anything this exciting in my life," Taylor protested.

Matthias smiled, the first and last we were likely to see.

"When the Mars colony was built, a powerful AI was built to act as a warden and protector. In the wake of a terrible civil war, the AI became more autocratic and protective. It lost its ability to feel compassion, even the programmed kind. While it continues to serve its purpose, it is anything but a beneficent patron of the Martian people."

"I'm from Mars?" she asked incredulously.

"No, but when the Lunar Colony was built it was given a mother and a father AI to balance them out," Matthias said. "In the wake of that, the two believed they needed to create children that could journey to earth, learn what it is to be human, and eventually return home to share what they learned. In this way, the two AIs could stay balanced and benevolent protectors of the Lunar peoples."

"So, I'm a moon baby?" Taylor replied, still skeptical.

"You're a countermeasure, but 'moon baby' works too," Matthias said with a half-smile.

"How do you know all this?"

Matthias paused for a moment. He seemed to collect his thoughts before speaking.

"I contributed most of the code that comprises the intelligent agent on Mars and the pair on the Lunar Colony. My contribution to the MDC Project had to do with artificial intelligence as well," Matthias said.

"So, you're like my grandpa?" Taylor said with an impish smile.

"I never really thought of it that way, but yes," Matthias replied attempting in vain to defend himself from Taylor as she flew across the table to hug him.

"Will my parents love me when I come home?"

Matthias paused again, trying to summon the proper words.

"They can't right now. Not yet. You'll have to show them how. None of their children have returned yet, and if Madmar has his way, none of them ever will."

Taylor turned and looked at me, then turned her gaze back to Silverstein. Her eyes filled with tears, and she began to weep bitterly while Matthias did his best to comfort her.

Silverstein's turned to me and narrowed his eyes angrily. I nodded to him, as if to say I had his back.

"I promised Taylor I wouldn't let anything happen to her. Being cut off from her home on the Lunar colony as a result of an economic apocalypse on Earth certainly qualifies. What do we need to do to stop this?" Silverstein said.

"We may need the catalyst you left in Port Montaigne. Once we have it, and have verified it is what we believe it to be, we need to get it, Taylor, and the code, to Helsinki. If we can get them all to the CGG Mainframe, we might be able to limit the damage Madmar has arranged using the CGG's greed and Vance's network," Matthias replied, a tone of urgency creeping into his voice.

"There's no way we can go back to Port Montaigne right now, and there are rubber coated goons all over downtown looking for us," Taylor said.

Matthias and Silverstein exchanged knowing glances. She was right, getting the catalyst back would be extremely difficult. None of them could get into the downtown area and out again without encountering serious trouble.

"I'll get the catalyst. You guys start figuring out how we're getting to Helsinki," I stated grimly.

"Ezra, if they catch you, they'll kill you," Silverstein said, shaking his head.

"You have a better plan? I'm listening," I replied as I gestured to my own pointed ears.

They didn't have a better plan. Matthias would arrange to have one of his flight capable prototypes drop me into midtown. From there, I would have to sneak down into the downtown area and find where Taylor and Silverstein hid the catalyst.

I knew it would take every trick I knew to get in there. I couldn't help but think about the last time the catalyst was used on Taylor. It gave her incredible power, allowing her to move faster than a bullet.

If just an ounce injected into her has that kind of effect, what would she be capable of with a full suite of those chemicals at our disposal? I just hoped whatever Matthias planned to use the catalyst for wouldn't hurt Taylor.

Because if it did, I would kill him.

CHAPTER 11

Rural Georgia – Matthias's Hideout

6:45 AM, December 27th, 2199

Ezra's War Journal Part 2

After plotting a course and figuring out the best ground route to take, Matthias and I decided the best way was to air drop me into midtown. He said he had a vehicle that could do the job, getting me both in and out once I'd acquired the catalyst. Silverstein and Taylor both disliked the idea but they could offer no alternative.

Matthias took several moments preparing a small transport, air-capable, and totally silent, or so I was told. It looked more like a satellite or an escape pod as opposed to a vehicle but he assured me, several times, without prompting, that it was completely safe. Not the worst thing I'd ever been stuffed into.

I climbed inside Matthias's sleek looking contraption as he explained that it had been designed to find military personnel on the ground, and deliver supplies to them. He called it a "Canary." The traveling compartment would have been beyond cramped for anyone but me.

I mourned the fact that there was no window, making the contraption feel like a coffin from the inside. I figured I'd use the solitude to quietly focus on what I was about to do. For certain, it wouldn't be a sightseeing trip by any stretch.

"Ready?" Matthias inquired as he made sure I was strapped in tightly.

"Tell me what to do again, after I've got the catalyst?" I asked, looking over at Silverstein and Taylor.

"Use your mobile to send Taylor a message. Once it's received I'll have the Canary that brought you figure out where you are, and pick you up." Matthias replied.

"Why Taylor's mobile?"

"Silverstein's assumption about her ability to impart an almost unbreakable level of encryption to devices in her possession is correct. Any message routed through her mobile, so long as it is in her possession, cannot be traced. Understand?" Matthias explained again for the fourth time.

I understood completely, but really enjoyed the look on Taylor's face whenever someone related how special she was. She was so pleased to be able to help in some way. It was worth making both Matthias and Silverstein crazy by acting forgetful about her abilities.

"You sure about this? We could find another way..." Silverstein said kneeling down next to the hatch.

"We each have a contribution to make. Taylor may not be able to make hers without the Catalyst and there are millions of lives at stake. This is my contribution," I replied.

"Ezra, please don't die. Oh, and could you pick up some of my things while you're at my building?" Taylor said, sliding me an obscenely long list of her belongings.

"I'll see what I can do," I replied, winking at Silverstein.

Matthias closed the hatch. It was pitch black inside until the Canary's internal systems began to come online. Then, after the engine had powered up, the whole craft jerked upward violently. I nearly bit my tongue.

It was a maddening journey back across the land toward the Port. I couldn't see anything but I could feel myself and the Canary traveling at a very high rate of speed. Its engines chirped and sang, which I assumed was the reason Matthias gave it that name.

I hummed to myself while I waited. It was something I did back home in the underground when waiting for the cisterns and water chambers to shift. Just me, alone, in a tiny pipe, with millions of gallons of floodwaters rushing below me.

After what felt like hours, the Canary finally came to rest and disgorged me onto a rooftop in midtown. Shaking the fog from my head I looked around for a bit of loose roofing with which to obscure the contraption. From the rooftop I could see I was probably a three hour walk to Taylor's apartment building.

It was more or less what we'd planned.

The few people I came across in midtown ignored me as long as I kept my cowl up and my head down. I still had all the kitchen knives from the mansion stashed about my person. I hoped I wouldn't need them. I prayed that the mission could be achieved by stealth alone. At the time, I couldn't have known how much trouble and blood I was in for.

When I reached the seaside edge of the Port of Montaigne, it was clear the Collectors had been turning the place upside down looking for us. The streets were empty. I could see people hiding wherever they could, in abandoned buildings, overturned trash bins, and drainage tunnels.

They must have wanted us badly. Something we had or knew could still mess up whatever the master plan was. I felt bad that these humans had to suffer so terribly just because we left town. Hopefully all this blood would be worth it in the end.

There weren't many, but I could see and smell small cooking fires and hear the whispers of downtowners afraid to wander the streets. That last twenty-four hours had plunged the area into hell. I normally didn't feel bad when humans suffered, but having a few friends who were members of that race changed things for me.

After an hour of walking, I arrived at what Taylor called the strip, a portion of downtown with commercial spaces that still had power and services. The Strip and Waffle was one such place. There was a pawn shop, the strip club, a corner drug store, and a barber shop all around a single intersection.

The place looked like a war zone. Not a single business was open and the streets were littered with debris, smoldering vehicles, and overturned trash bins. There were bodies, too. At least a half dozen poor souls got caught in whatever violence had transpired.

From the looks of it, they only killed those who fought back. There was an old man with a shotgun, a woman beside him with a rolling pin. They died trying to protect the old man's barber shop. People do desperate things when you threaten to take the only thing they love away from them. I wanted with all my being to avenge them.

There were only a few shell casings, far less than there were bullet holes. Mercenaries, like the ones we met in the concrete factory, bearing similar weapons and training. I didn't dare break into the open, but it looked like they arrived in armored personnel transports, deployed, and began firing at the businesses specifically. Not a single one still had an unbroken window.

Nothing I could do there except say a short observance for the dead. We Drones do not believe in God per se, but we do believe there is something watching over us all. A benevolent force one cannot see but can instead feel in the warmth of camaraderie and community.

I wasted no time following the route I'd already worked out in my head. I paused near what I thought was an empty machine shop. I peeped through a shattered window where I saw several Martian mercenaries inside holding prisoners. Mostly women and children lay on their sides weeping while the armed individuals talked over payment with what I assumed were slavers.

The vision of the old barber and his wife flashed through my mind, and for a moment, I forgot the mission.

I walked the perimeter looking for sentries before sliding in through a shattered part of the foundation and moving toward them just beneath the floor. I could see them pacing above me as I reached an industrial drain under a lift. The drain was tight. I had to temporarily dislocate a shoulder to squeeze through. Watching and listening for a few moments from beneath an equipment lift, I listened to the mercenaries talk, and in a language I'd heard before. They were from off world.

One of them backed over toward me, leaning against the lift. I took advantage and clipped the back of his ankle with my claws. He cried out as he fell, reflexively pulling the trigger on his weapon. The slaver and his comrades opened fire on the mercenaries thinking some sort of double-cross was in progress.

I slid out on my belly amidst the chaos. Rolling over, I knocked out the only overhead light with one of the kitchen knives. I crouched down low and waited the two seconds it would take for my eyes to adjust to the darkness.

The firefight between the two groups was savage, but thankfully all at waist level. Captives let loose muffled cries as I wove my way through the shadows toward a female mercenary. She was about to turn her weapon downward toward the hostages. I grabbed the barrel of her weapon and held it aloft as I stabbed her again and again with my claws. Bullets tore through the air around me, her screams drowned out by the roar of automatic weapons.

Not many of them had survived, and I could see them weaving through the carnage and smoke toward me. I dodged behind one of the lifts and grabbed a handful of metal shavings from the ground. As the slaver came around to flank me, I hurled the shavings into his eyes, but to no avail, he was wearing eye protection. The butt of his rifle came down on me hard, then again, across my forehead. I pitched backward up against a work bench as he came at me again. He was trying to take me alive. Last mistake he would ever make.

Still angry as hell, I stepped into him, I brought my foot down on his lower leg, breaking his knee. He pitched forward across my shoulder as I brought my clawed hand up, disemboweling him. One of his remaining crew reached for his sidearm, but far too slowly as I hurled the slaver in him.

They both fell backward into a bloody heap. I made certain they were all dead save the one I left lying incapacitated beneath their dead ally. He was breathing heavily, unable to push the weight of their friend, and all the gear they carried. I knelt down so he could see my face.

"You had orders to capture and sell these poor people? What were they going to do, work the shafts on Mars?" I whispered.

The slaver looked up at me with his one good eye and winced.

"Not Mars, they were to all be shipped to Northern Canada, into the arctic region," he replied with a heavy Martian accent.

It struck me as odd that he'd give up that kind of intel without more arm twisting. He knew I wasn't letting him out of there alive. What he was telling me was just crazy enough to be the truth.

I made sure the slaver would never harm anyone again. Then, I began dragging the half dozen or so captives outside and releasing them. It would have been faster to release them inside, but they probably wouldn't have liked how I redecorated the room.

They said nothing to me as I cut their bonds. I was bloody, though, and must have looked like hell after what I did to the heartless bastards who were intent on selling them. Humans are a remorseless race from all observation. What they did to my people seems like a lesser sin than what they are inclined to do to each other.

Glad to be free of that situation, I rubbed my forehead where I'd taken the stroke from the rifle. Taking a moment to catch my breath, I sat on the curb between a wrecked vehicle and a pallet of moldering cardboard. I started thinking about the whole situation, always a mistake in my case. I'm a lot better at doing things than I ever was contemplating the big picture.

Even the rival tribe that fought with my own would respect us on the field and fight honorably, soldier to soldier. No women or kids, and we always gave each other mercy when we asked for it. Maybe this impending cataclysm was simply justice for what humanity had wrought upon the world? Maybe Silverstein thought the same before he lost his memory?

I would come to know these things in time.

Looking at the destruction and sorrow arrayed around me, it was clear that much of humanity was already bankrupt in the most important respects. Apparent as it was, it wasn't up to me to judge anyone. It wasn't like I sought the high road to solve my problems either.

I finished feeling sorry for myself, stood up, and began making my way back to Taylor's apartment building. The path I'd chosen allowed me to avoid the patrols and the trouble that came with them. Along the way, there were many signs that the mercs had been leaning on downtown, hard.

At last, I reached Taylor's building, which seemed relatively untouched by the chaos stretching back toward midtown. There didn't appear to be anyone around the apartment building, but I could smell them. I could smell their synthetic poly-Kevlar woven body armor, the fishy smelling gun oil on their weapons, and the fear coming off their bodies.

It should have occurred to me that the mercenaries back at the machine shop might have had radios on them. There were piles of trash and other debris around the apartment complex, plenty of places they could be hiding. Wherever they were, they were close.

There were two ways I could have played it, and all my plans went right out the window when I saw Dr. Helmet making his way toward the apartment complex. I couldn't let him get killed, so I broke cover and sprinted out toward him. He turned, somewhat surprised as I came out of the darkness, motioning for him to follow.

"Helmet, quickly, we've got to get out of here," I whispered.

Helmet nodded and ran toward me, looking around nervously. I didn't even see it coming, no warning or provocation. Helmet closed the distance and kicked me hard, harder than any human had right to. The blow dislodged two of my ribs and sent me flying over into the side of a wrecked vehicle.

Helmet walked calmly over beside where I lay. I coughed up blood as I tried to right myself. All I could manage to do was sit up and try like hell to breathe.

"Sorry about that Ezra, but I'm curious, why did you come back here?" Dr. Helmet asked, as Martian mercenaries gathered around him.

"Taylor-- she forgot-- her pink shoes, grabbed--purple by mistake," I said, gasping for air.

"You sure? What about these?" Helmet said, holding up the small box that contained the catalyst.

"Helmet, why? Why are you doing this?"

"Helmet? Oh, he's been dead for almost a year. My name is Madmar, Dr. Maurice Madmar."

Things all snapped into place. I couldn't understand at the time why I'd been so unwilling to trust Helmet, some part of me could sense that he was lying. Deep down in my guts, I knew he was a fraud.

I snapped up to my feet, leaping just high enough to avoid the machine gun fire, to the top of the wrecked vehicle behind me. My entire body ached. Running on adrenaline alone, I knew I wasn't good for too much more of this type of action. A stray bullet bounced off the ground, up through the vehicle, and pierced my right foot.

Dropping to all fours, my body screamed for oxygen as I leapt at Madmar. I took half his face off as I pulled him to the ground. I didn't even care if I died anymore. I had to put a stop to him. The mercs rushed in to stop me as I raked my claws back and forth across his face and throat.

Then the smell hit me. That sickening machine smell that Matthias exposed me to. This thing I'd just killed wasn't really Madmar or Helmet, but a synthetic stand in. I grabbed the box out of his hand as the mercs got to me and opened it.

Empty.

They started kicking and hitting me mercilessly. I pulled my arms and legs up, curling into a ball, trying feebly to protect myself from the blows. I could hear them shouting at me, calling me a freak and worse.

I thought I was going to die.

Machine gun fire broke out, but not the same type as the weapons the mercenaries carried. Bullets streaked over me, tearing into the mercenaries. They turned to return fire as a rocket propelled grenade hit their transport.

I could hear them calling out on their radios as they returned fire. There was little I could do but lay there in the dirt and play dead. The exchange lasted less than two minutes, with the mercenaries running away in the face of what I could hear was greater firepower.

Booted feet walked past me in the gravel as nearly two dozen individuals stepped over and around me.

"Who's this little guy?"

"Ezra, I think that's his name," Officer Collins said turning me over.

Collins and a handful of men stood there gazing down at me. I could also see Taylor's boss from the Strip and Waffle and the man who managed her apartment building. They were heavily armed, and the uniformed Officer Collins usually wore was lacking the badge it displayed last time I saw him.

It all felt and smelled wrong. Even the hardest mercenary stinks of fear in a fire fight, but none of them gave off a single pheromone's worth. I thought, in that moment, it was just because I was hurt so bad, my own adrenaline reaction masking what my senses would normally detect. I tried to speak, but a terrible pain wracked my body with even the slightest movements. Collins gathered me up in his arms and carried me back to where they'd parked a couple of transports. Most of the people walking back looked like regular people, folks who took up weapons to protect their home.

Collins laid me down just inside the larger of the two transports where a woman began trying to patch me up. She was dressed in a clean white coat, had manicured nails, smelled of some kind of perfume, and her hair was nicely done up. She was an uptown dweller from the look and smell of her. I could smell her just fine, but not the others.

Collins sat down next to me, his legs dangling down the boarding ramp into the transport. He motioned to the others, and they dashed off in response, to secure the perimeter or some nonsense. I breathed a little easier now, but my adrenaline was still going.

"They came down here about twenty four hours ago looking for Taylor and Silverstein, but mostly for Taylor," Collins said, lighting a hand-rolled cigarette.

I turned and looked at him, to let him know I could hear him.

"Joe over at the Strip and Waffle started handing out guns, Russ opened up a couple of lids so we could use the tunnels, and I started organizing willing individuals to resist them. No way were we going to let downtown get steamrolled by these out-of-towners without a fight," Collins said.

I nodded.

"Is Taylor safe?" Collins asked.

I nodded again.

"In the first couple of hours, it was like a turf war, and we took our wounded to Helmet. We showed back up to find our wounded euthanized, and the doctor was gone. I'm the one that took Silverstein to Dr. Helmet when I first found him," Collins lamented.

The nurse finished patching me up, giving me a shot of stimulants. My already powerful metabolism was working overtime to repair my broken body. I sat up slowly, popping my jaw back into place, and looked over at Collins.

"You took Silverstein to Helmet?" I whispered.

"Yeah."

"If that's true, why should I trust you now?"

"I just saved your ass."

"Yep, pretty convenient you being here. I have always been lucky, though," I said looking at Collins.

Collins nodded, turning toward me a moment too late. I hit him as hard as I could, sending him head over heels out of the transport. The blow should have killed him, but he was already trying to regain his footing. I grabbed the nurse and tossed her out the back on top of him.

"Lucky, I'm not a fool," I growled angrily.

Before they could right themselves, I mashed the ramp control button, closing the transport. They banged on the outside of the ramp, angrily hurling insults and worse. I leaned heavily against the interior wall, exhausted, and checked my bandages while I had the chance.

I pulled a tracking device the "nurse" had planted on me and crushed it. The device was Martian technology, bulky and crude compared to what one could find on Earth. The whole set up had been almost perfect. Might have actually fallen for it if they'd found someone from downtown to play the part of the nurse.

If they'd wired me up, there was no reason Madmar didn't slip one inside Silverstein while he was patching him up. Or was there? That is, unless he was worried about Matthias finding it when they eventually met. It meant that my own home underground, the water tower Matthias converted into a hideout, all possibly compromised. To my core, I'm a warrior. I've never been one for thinking, but I resolved to give it my best shot after I'd made sure it would be a little harder to follow me.

I leapt into the cockpit and grabbed the controls. I'd watched Silverstein do this enough to know I didn't have a prayer of getting this VTOL transport off the ground. Fortunately, that was not my intent.

The larger transport lurched violently forward into the smaller one, wrecking it. The impact was enough to break the thick, laminated glass windshields in the transport I'd hijacked. More angry screams came from outside as machine gun fire bounced off the armored exterior.

I kicked the corner window out and slid to the ground quietly as the transport's engines continued to strain, pushing it further into the ground. I could hear the pop of artillery fire behind me lighting up the transport. The concussion from the explosion carried me to the ground beneath the remains of the VTOLs.

They searched for me in vain, sifting through the wreckage, trying to confirm the kill. I inched away from them, a mound of debris at a time until I was clear. From a distance I could see they were extremely angry about not being able to dupe or kill me.

Their plan was falling apart.

That's when it hit me. Madmar hadn't bugged Silverstein, that's why he'd set up this elaborate ruse. Why would they tear up downtown if they already knew where Silverstein was? He must have known I wouldn't give up their location to him, no matter how much he tortured me.

Madmar gambled that I'd give the intel up to a friend. I was a little bit scared of what he'd do now, even as I struggled to figure out what his true motivations were. My mobile had been smashed, which meant I had to get back to the Canary to warn Silverstein and Taylor.

That was a long walk, as beat up as I was.

I watched from the rooftop as Collins and his crew wandered about below looking for me and a new set of wheels. Russ had been far enough down in the tunnels to possibly figure out where my home was. I was torn between getting to a communications device and killing someone that might lead evil men back to my home.

In the end, I decided to split the difference and take a terrible risk.

I spent the next hour stalking Russ while allowing my body to heal. I could feel my bones and muscles knitting back together, bruises vanishing, and lacerations closing. I was so tired.

Near an old bodega at the edge of the crumbling tourist district, Russ wandered into an alley to smoke. I dropped silently from the rooftop to the alley floor beside him. He fumbled for his weapon, the cigarette tumbling out of his mouth. I punched him in the solar plexus as hard as I could.

He doubled over gasping for air as I clawed the strap running from his rifle over his shoulder. I put the rifle down on the top of a rusted dumpster quietly as I squatted next to him. He fell to one side, clutching his stomach and continued gasping for air.

"Why, Russ? What did Taylor ever do to you, that made it seem alright to do this to her?" I questioned.

Russ struggled for air for a moment before he could reply.

"I'm not really here. I'm hanging suspended in a tube of liquid somewhere, wired up to control a plastic version of myself. Madmar said I could have my real body back if I did what I was told."

"What about Officer Collins and the others?"

"Not sure. They might be in the same mess I'm in. We all got rounded up in the last week or so I think, told that we'd have to..."

Russ started to scream, but I muffled him with my hand, pushing the tip of one of my claws into his eyelid. He immediately stopped screaming, but I could see he was in terrible agony.

"What is it?" I asked.

"I can feel what he's doing to my body. Punishing me for talking to you," Russ said.

"Why is he doing this? Where is your body?" I asked, turning Russ's face toward my own.

Russ struggled to talk, the faint smell of burning bio-electric components wafting out of his mouth. I watched silently, completely helpless, as he suffered. Servos and other mechanical parts deep inside Russ's false body seized as the real Russ died a painful death somewhere miles and miles away.

I turned what was left of him over and searched for a mobile. He had two. One was brand new, only two numbers in the contact list. The other was old and beat to hell, a couple dozen numbers stored inside. I opted for the old beat to hell one, less likely it was one Madmar had issued to his cronies.

I clicked it open and dialed Taylor's mobile. Barely half a ring later, I could hear her voice on the other end. I looked down at the display of the mobile and watched the screen go blank for a moment as Taylor unconsciously took control of the device.

"Ezra! Are you okay? Why are you calling me from Russ's mobile?" Taylor asked.

"Where are you?"

"We're still at the water tank laboratory place with Matthias. Where's Russ, is he there with you?"

I didn't know what to say.

"What's wrong Ezra?" She asked.

I struggled to pull the events of the last few hours together. How could I tell her that Madmar had kidnapped everyone she and Silverstein knew and forced them to remotely control synthetic copies of themselves while their real bodies were held hostage? How could I tell her Russ was dead and Madmar was abducting people and taking them to the Canadian tundra?

"Things are really messed up here. I need to get back so I can explain what's happened," I said.

"You sound different. Are you hurt?"

"Yeah, but I heal quick. I've got nothing but bad news, and I wasn't able to lay hands on the catalyst either."

Taylor went silent on the other end for a moment.

"I don't understand, Ezra. It wasn't where Silverstein and I left it?"

"Taylor, down here nothing is where you guys left it," I replied.

"What about my stuff? How much were you able to grab off the list I gave you?" she joked.

It was more than I could bear. I wept bitterly on the mobile while Taylor listened. It felt like I'd let everyone down and nothing I did thereafter would matter. Then, I heard Silverstein's voice come across the mobile.

"Ezra, tell me what's going on down there," Silverstein said.

I told him everything, including the bit about Madmar and his synthetic body double shell game. I told him about Russ and about how the catalyst and a bunch of people were probably hidden out in the arctic.

"I'm sorry about the catalyst," I said.

"Forget the catalyst. You got us something more important," Silverstein replied.

"Information," I said.

"Exactly. Hard to say exactly what Madmar's game is, but we know three times what we did a few hours ago. Thank you, Ezra," Silverstein said.

A game. That is exactly what this seemed to be. I wondered if the catalyst was just more poison, meant to control Taylor and others like her, assuming there were any others. I hoped we weren't making a mistake giving up on recovering it, but I was more than ready to quit stumbling into Madmar's traps and minions.

"What's our next move?" I said.

"You get the heck out of there, that's what. We'll figure out what to do next once you're safely out of there. Matthias says the Canary should be there in a couple minutes," Silverstein said.

I made sure no one was about before I started to make the climb back to the bodega's roof. Silverstein stayed on the line relaying the Canary's proximity to me as it got closer. I hung up with him as it broke the roofline in the distance slowing to descend on my position.

"See you soon."

CHAPTER 12

Rural Georgia – Matthias's Hideout

9:13 AM, December 28th, 2199

Ezra's War Journal Part 3

The Canary sped me back across the seaboard toward where Matthias and my friends were holed up. The journey gave me time to heal, and think. At the time, I was pretty sure intel on both Finland and Arctic were setups. Madmar probably had plans inside of plans.

I hoped that between Matthias and Silverstein and what I'd told them, they'd have something figured out by the time I showed up. The whole thing struck me as odd, replaying what had happened over and over again in my mind. It was almost as though Madmar was doing this just to hurt Taylor.

The Canary came to a rest at last. The hatch opened and harsh artificial light spilled across the interior. I got a look at myself for the first time following all the action I saw in downtown Port Montaigne. I looked like hell.

"Oh my God, Ezra! What did they do to you?" Taylor exclaimed as she wrapped her arms around me.

"I'm okay. You should have seen the other guys."

Taylor helped me out onto the concrete floor of the area Matthias stored all his vehicles. I looked around for Silverstein and Matthias, but we were alone. Taylor helped me to my feet and frowned at me.

"No, I didn't bring any of your stuff. Didn't even make it inside the building," I said.

"It's okay. I can always get more stuff. You're a little harder to replace," Taylor said.

It was good to be wanted. We walked the narrow walkways back toward the laboratory proper. Taylor was her usual bubbly and optimistic self along the way, but it did little to throw salve on my worry. I assumed Silverstein hadn't told her what happened to Russ.

We entered the laboratory and made our way down to the work tables arrayed at the center. Silverstein and Matthias sat at one of the tables chatting quietly. I could tell by their expressions they weren't expecting to see me so torn up.

"Ezra--"

"I'm fine. What's the plan, Silverstein?"

"Matthias thinks Madmar has a self-sustainable facility up in the Arctic. He's probably got contingencies set up there to make sure this economic shutdown goes down even if someone gets to the CGG servers in Finland."

"Does he?" I replied, somewhat sarcastically.

Silverstein was somewhat taken back by my tone and looked back at Matthias. Matthias lowered his head, putting his hand head in hands before responding to my accusatory glare.

"I know he has a facility," Matthias replied wearily. "There were a few isolated incidents with the MDC Project during the war. One resulted in an Arctic facility going dark. A team of Orbital Response Marines were dropped in, but were never heard from again"

Silverstein turned and looked at Matthias, somewhat surprised. Then he said what I was already thinking.

"Matthias, what is it you're not telling us?" Silverstein demanded. "What is this really about?"

Matthias rubbed his chin, now covered with stubble and blinked his tired eyes at us. "This has always been about Taylor, I think."

"Wait, I don't understand," Taylor said, looking at Matthias.

I walked slowly over to Matthias so I was standing right next to him and let my claws slowly slide out, clicking into place. Matthias just hung his head.

"Madmar needs Taylor to hack the orbital relays and the Moon Colony," Matthias explained. "I've already seen to it that Mars and the outlying colonies are beyond his reach, for now. He's doing this to hurt Dr. Helmet and me for pushing him out of the MDC Project."

I bristled at the thought of anyone trying to hurt Taylor while simultaneously trying to grasp whether Matthias was a friend or an enemy.

"I should have killed Madmar when I had the chance, years ago. I knew he would never let this go. Every time he looks up into the night sky he sees what Helmet and I intended to leave behind as our legacy. He means to corrupt and control the two Lunar Control AIs," Matthias said.

"And he will watch the world burn, consumed in this economic catastrophe in the process?" Silverstein asked.

"You tell me, you're the one that set it all up," Matthias replied coldly.

"Helmet is dead. Been dead at least a year if Madmar was telling the truth," I said.

"No. Like everything, that too must be a lie. There's no way he would kill Helmet before he'd taken control of the Lunar Control AIs. He wants Helmet and I to both see our creation taken from us and used for his own twisted purposes," Matthias said.

I shook my head at the thought of what sort of madness could consume a person and allow them to seek vengeance in this way. At the time I had no idea how evil Madmar was, or what he was willing to do in order to achieve his goals. I still thought I was dealing with a human that had lost his way. What Matthias told us next was the first real hint at what sort of monster we were dealing with.

"The classified war and the invasion, does Madmar have the tech to fake something like that?" Silverstein asked.

"Yes. It would have fooled everyone except for a self-contained intelligent agent with access to their own satellite array," Matthias admitted.

"How many people died in this fake war no one but CGG officials knew about?" Taylor asked.

"Hundreds of thousands, sent into space to die or starve. I can't be sure honestly," Matthias asked.

"Meanwhile, you sat here and did nothing?" Silverstein said, shaking his head.

"No, not nothing. I couldn't let on that either I or the Lunar AI array knew anything about it. All I could do was try to expose CGG's involvement to the right people. I looked for other idealistic individuals with the skills to pull the rug out from under the whole thing," Matthias said.

"People like Vance Uroboros, A.K.A., Silverstein," Taylor said, finding a seat at the table.

Matthias nodded solemnly. "I suppose, but Vance appeared to be at the game longer than I."

"When were you going to tell us all this?" I flexed my claws.

"I wasn't. I hoped that none of it would come to light until Taylor returned to the parent AIs on the moon. I was just trying to protect her," Matthias said.

"You'd burn Silverstein and me to do that?" I growled turning my back to Matthias.

"Taylor eventually returning home is far more important than any one or two people's lives," Matthias said.

"Glad you feel that way," I said before leaping on Matthias.

I took him out of his chair to the ground and wrapped one of my clawed hands around his throat.

"No!" Taylor protested, grabbing me around the arm.

Silverstein pulled her away as I turned my attention back to Matthias. He didn't struggle, just laid there, looking up into my eyes. I nicked him across his cheek, taking in the aroma of his blood.

"It's really you, and not some synthetic body double. That's a bad move if you were planning on double-crossing us," I said, looking over at Silverstein.

"A really bad move. If that were my plan, or if I operated like Madmar," Matthias replied calmly.

I got down off Matthias and helped him up. He stood up and dusted himself off as Taylor breathed a sigh of relief. Silverstein came over beside me, putting his hand on my shoulder. In hindsight, it was good to know someone had my back.

"Okay, Grampa, how do we stop Madmar, keep him from hurting any more people?" Taylor asked.

"We kill him," Silverstein replied.

Matthias stood there, lost in thought for a moment, before nodding his assent. Taylor looked around in disbelief for a moment before storming over toward the door. Just before she hit the door, she turned and shot us a glance that made me wither.

"Isn't killing Madmar going to make us no better than he is?" Taylor scolded.

Silverstein and Matthias just looked up at her, both unmoved by her question.

"Remember Russ, the guy who managed your apartment building? Madmar tortured and killed him," I said. "He's probably got Officer Collins, your boss Joe, and a few dozen other of your neighbors."

Taylor stared at me angrily for a moment.

"It's only murder when a human kills another human. This will be a Drone, a broken down old scientist, a terrestrial AI, and an amnesiac killing a monster. Madmar is a blight, even by downtown standards," I said shaking my head.

Taylor's expression softened as she began to understand that we were trying to protect her.

"What else haven't you guys told me about what happened while Ezra was on safari in downtown Port Montaigne?" Taylor sighed.

I availed her of everything Silverstein was too soft-hearted to tell her. I described the look in Russ's eyes. I gave her the details of the guilt he felt betraying his friend, and the terrible agony he felt before he died. I told her that my home, the place she'd lovingly decorated, and the rest of downtown, and the world, would not be safe as long as Madmar lived.

"Why are you telling me all this?" Taylor said, tears appearing in the corners of her eyes.

"He wants you to know so that you can tell your mom and dad when you go home to the moon. They need to be warned," Silverstein said, pulling out one of his special cigarettes.

"I'm not going home, I'm going with you guys," Taylor said pointing a finger at us.

"No, they're right. It might be the only way to protect you and the Lunar AIs, your mother and father, from Madmar," Matthias said, turning his chair upright and sitting down in it.

"I don't ditch on my friends, so you can forget that noise!" Taylor growled.

Matthias pushed components from a screen on one of the table. He pressed a couple of buttons on the side causing the ceramic clad display to hum to life. He brought up a full color topographical of the world that showed every hill and valley, the position of day and night, and the path of certain satellites in orbit.

We gathered around the table quietly as he pulled up his data slate and started entering in information. Two areas on the map lit up, a point in the Arctic and one in Finland. We gazed at the two points unsure of what we were seeing.

"These translucent lines passing over these two points are orbitals critical to Earth's defenses. Madmar was able to push through having them built in the wake of the war with alien invaders. These two points, the Arctic base and the CGG's server farm in Finland are nexus points where, every 24 hours, these satellites pass overhead," Matthias said in a hushed tone.

"There are gaps. Points when the satellites aren't overhead and he can't see what's happening. Moments of sensory darkness," Silverstein remarked after a few moments watching the patterns.

"You're pretty good. Took me a day or two to figure that out, but you can tell just from looking a few moments," Matthias replied.

"Naw, I was just guessing," Silverstein replied with a smile.

"Right. The windows of sensory darkness do not correspond and there isn't enough time elapsed between the two, even in my fastest transport, to get between both places in the same twenty-four hour period," Matthias said.

"We'll have to split up," I said.

"Madmar is my problem, always was. I'll go to the Arctic and try to deal with him. You three need to head to Finland. If Silverstein and Taylor can get access to the server farm, they might be able to avert this tragedy," Matthias said.

"Won't we need the catalyst?" Silverstein asked.

"The catalyst helps her to do things she can already do on her own. Taylor, you haven't scratched the surface of your abilities. Given the right motivation, I have faith you'll come through."

"That stuff I was injected with, that made me run really fast, was that a result of the catalyst?" Taylor asked.

"I have similar questions about the catalyst as it was not of my design. Maybe it's simply another lie to obscure Madmar's true motivations?" Matthias mused, motioning for his digital assistant to bring him a data slate.

"I hadn't thought of this before, but like any computer, and the human body itself, there will be a sort of record of all she has endured, maybe even a log," Matthias held up his data slate, pressing the palm of Taylor's hand to the glass display. After a few moments he reviewed the data. He smiled slightly as he slid the data over to Silverstein.

"Catalyst is a misnomer, one that even misled Madmar's own unwitting agents. It was a sort of virus, written to take control of you," Silverstein said after reviewing the collected data.

"While I can't discern the catalyst's exact nature, it apparently failed to override your free will. Your own body does keep a sort of log detailing the basic responses to everything it encounters, probably to add to your findings when you return home to the Lunar AIs. They tried to take control of you and the nano-machines that comprise your body deployed powerful countermeasures to protect itself. Even collecting this data was difficult, requiring software I wrote myself," Matthias continued, reviewing the information displayed on his data slate.

"Why would they need so much catalyst if they were just trying to control Taylor?" I asked, already knowing the answer.

"I suspect as you do, that Taylor is not the only terrestrial intelligent agent left wandering the Earth. Others must have survived," Matthias replied.

"You've only got one Transport down there Matthias, and I don't think you're going to ride in the Canary all the way to the Arctic," I said.

Matthias nodded. Taking back his data slate he tapped across the screen. Red warning lights began to flash as a section of ceiling opened up. A lift began to descend, bearing a large suit of matte black powered armor to the laboratory floor.

"What is it?" Taylor asked, putting her hand on the suit.

"S-AC Aquiline Class Jump Trooper Combat Suit, designed by Victor Seraphim," Matthias said looking up at the ominous hunk of metal. "It is a sleeker version of the S-A0, outfitted with a refraction field, and modified for stealth. It's completely invisible on radar and thermal imaging. Silent as a ghost, the joints collectively moving to produce less than three decibels of sound. The suit provides the wearer with increased strength allowing the use of heavy weapons. It comes standard with thermal imaging, light amplification, laser targeting technology, a fully encrypted communications system, and an AI based computer system that warns the user of dangers while automatically redirecting the refraction fields to intercept incoming attacks. Victor Seraphim only manufactured one hundred of these special suits. Less than twenty five survived the war."

"You'll need it if you plan on taking Madmar by yourself," Silverstein remarked.

"It's a one way trip. I don't plan on coming back," Matthias stated plainly.

Taylor looked back at him, her face filling with worry.

"If we fail and this economic disaster takes place, the world will need Mechanics, tele-mechanical psychics like yourself, to put the world back together again. I don't see how this is a good plan," Silverstein said.

"Agreed," Taylor and I said almost at the same time.

"My choice," Matthias said heading up the stairs.

"Where are you going?" Taylor asked.

"To suit up, we've got precious little time," Matthias said, exiting the laboratory.

Silverstein furrowed his brow in deep thought, trying like he usually did to put all the variables into place. He turned to Taylor and I pulling out his mobile. He waited for a moment then started scrolling through some text on the display.

"You guys trust Matthias?" Silverstein said.

"Nope," I replied without hesitation.

"I don't know," Taylor said with great trepidation in her voice.

"There's nothing in the news about what happened in Downtown. There's not even a blurb. What if we are underestimating Madmar and our role in all this? He could have key individuals around the globe replaced with synthetic replicas, and a lot more control over the situation than we realize," Silverstein remarked.

"What makes you think that?" Taylor asked.

"It's what I would have done in his position. Heck, it's probably what I did do by cloning myself. I've been trying to figure out why I had so many clones set up to age at different rates. At some point I had his whole game figured out," Silverstein rambled angrily.

"That is weird," I replied.

"Unless, the clones being different ages wasn't intentional. There is some piece of this puzzle that just doesn't fit. One of these things is not like the others," Silverstein said while he paced back and forth.

"It's time to quit thinking about what Madmar might be doing and worry about what we are going to do. I suggest we get whatever we think we'll need, get on the transport and head to Finland, and try to put a stop to this mess," Taylor said.

She was right. We couldn't keep trying to grasp for direction through unknowable things. We started going through the laboratory and the vehicle warehouse for supplies. Then, we went out and picked enough fresh fruit and vegetables to last us the trip and beyond.

"Ezra, ever seen a carrot pulled straight from the ground like this?" she asked.

"No. Generally, all we Drones find are the peelings and the bits people didn't want," I said.

Silverstein and I carried stuff to the transport while Taylor sorted the junk from the good stuff. We grabbed a few extra sets of clothes. Didn't hurt my feelings as my old outfit was completely torn up from the last action I saw.

The transport already had several cases on board, locked in with a small front loader. We didn't bother to unload or inspect the cases. Looked like some sort of scientific equipment.

Silverstein sat down in the cockpit and began running diagnostics. Taylor and I looked on as he did an engine check and something else I didn't quite comprehend with the onboard computer. Taylor jumped into the co-pilot's position and immediately set about adjusting the seat.

"I'm pretty sure I can fly this thing. Strange. It almost seems familiar somehow," Silverstein said flipping some switches across the top panel.

"Out of everything we've seen and experienced, this feels familiar?" Taylor asked.

"You probably did a lot of traveling before you lost your memory, if half of what you're alleged to have done is true."

"You're probably right, Ezra," Silverstein replied heading back out to the landing.

We returned to the laboratory where Matthias had already set about prepping the suit of armor. I couldn't help but marvel at the sight of it, all matte black, sleek, and deadly as hell. Like me, it was made by humans for a purpose. I wondered if the onboard AI knew more about its purpose than I did about mine.

"Sorry, Ezra, I've only got the one," Matthias joked.

"It's okay, doubt they come in my size."

I laughed. It had been a long time since I'd done that. I wanted to again, once this was all over.

"Find your way around the transport?" Matthias asked.

"Yeah, I think it'll get us to Finland. We're going to come for you after we're done there. We won't leave you in the Arctic," Silverstein said.

"You guys worry about getting yourselves to safety in the aftermath. If I fail and Madmar slips away, he'll try to kill you two and take Taylor. We can't let that happen, understand?" Matthias said, suddenly more serious than I'd ever seen him.

"If she can teach the Lunar Central AIs about humanity, she also possesses the codes to access their core programming," Silverstein ventured.

"Yes, which is why Madmar can never, ever lay hands on her," Matthias said.

"Why are the Lunar AIs so important?" I asked Matthias.

"It would take too long to explain, and we're short on time. All I can say is that they are what will allow the world to survive the future," he stated plainly.

We said our goodbyes to Matthias, but not before Taylor took a few moments to talk to him. Silverstein and I gave her a moment and stepped out. When she was finished, we walked back to the vehicle warehouse and made our final preparations to leave.

I found a seat just behind the cockpit and made myself at home. The new pants and sweater Taylor had found for me were much warmer than my old outfit. I decided to catch some sleep and passed out before we even left the hangar.

When I awoke a couple of hours later we were still over the ocean. I looked out the small window on the side of the transport. I hoped to see a whale, a boat, or something but was disappointed.

"We're circling around north of British airspace. If you want a glimpse of the northern Scandinavian coastline you will want to look out the right hand side in about forty-five minutes," Silverstein said.

"We going to be okay to land?" Taylor asked.

"Yeah, we have a registered flight plan as a private charter. Since we aren't unloading anything but passengers, we only need to meet briefly with customs," he replied.

I was anxious about the whole thing, to tell the truth. I hadn't been walking distance away from the tunnels beneath the Port Montaigne for decades. Visiting a foreign country that may or may not have tunnels weighed heavily on my mind.

Taylor and I squeezed both our faces into the window as the coastline came into sight. It was nothing but ice, mountains, and a few trees. It was beautiful, and at the same time, I wondered if Taylor had packed us warm enough coats.

After passing over snowy forested areas for almost an hour, we finally came upon a large metropolitan area unlike anything I'd ever seen. The buildings were nowhere near as tall as the ones in Port Montaigne, and the whole of the place probably housed no more than a couple million people. Tiny when compared to the city that lurked above my home.

Silverstein put the transport down in a landing zone that was little more than a clearing amidst a grove of tall fir trees. There was an ancient four-wheeled vehicle and a small office sitting between the landing zone and a well maintained dirt road. An elderly gentlemen waved us down.

We exited the transport carrying one suitcase each. The elderly gentlemen greeted us with a thick accent and told us our cabin was ready and that he could take us up at our leisure. Silverstein nodded and let the old guy pack our luggage to the open-topped vehicle that awaited us.

"I can carry my own bag," I hissed at Silverstein.

"If we don't let him help, we can't tip him after we get to the cabin. We have to assume we're being watched at all times, maybe even from orbit," Silverstein whispered.

I felt a little foolish. Looking over at Taylor, I could tell she was more or less of the same opinion. We'd always done for ourselves, and no one carried our weight. We were too used to carrying our own.

The trees, pathway, and small animals we saw along the way to the cabin were captivating. I began wishing I had pencil and paper to sketch some of what I saw. Then I saw Taylor using her mobile to take a few pictures. Realizing I had my own, I did the same, nearly running out of memory. I planned to sort the pictures later.

"Here we are," Silverstein said, pointing to a cabin at the top of a hill.

The small vehicle that carried us there seemed to have no trouble making the climb. There were two more such vehicles, in much better condition parked outside.

"Is there someone already here?" Taylor asked.

Our elderly escort told us they were part of the rental and that we needed only plug them back in to recharge the batteries before we left. Silverstein seemed giddy at the prospect of roaring around on the trails in one. I couldn't tell if it was genuine or just part of pretending to be a tourist.

He unlocked the front door for us and handed Silverstein the keys. Then, he wished us all a good day and departed down the road. When he was safely out of sight, we went inside and swept for bugs as best we could, the layer of dust a safe indication no one had been inside for some time.

Taylor and Silverstein hadn't slept on the way and were visibly exhausted. They drew the shades and each grabbed a couch. I stood by the door for a moment, then slipped back outside quietly. I wanted to look around.

I walked the path to a small stream running down the hill, twisting between rocks and trees. I knelt there and did the most extraordinary thing. I put my hand in the ice cold water and watched as tiny particles of silt flowed past my hand. I would have admitted it to no one until now, but I thought I felt the land breathing around me. The wind spread kinetic force to the trees that seemed to transfer it to the ground and so forth. It was similar to the hum one felt putting your hand on a thermal core deep beneath a city. It was like a sort of warmth spreading out into the ground and into everything connected to it.

We Drones had always been taught there was nothing beyond the cities for us, that the ebb and flow within the under-tunnels was all we needed to sustain ourselves. There was so much about what I was that had been a lie. It is as they say, the truth really did set me free, in an odd sort of way. I was no longer confined to the under-tunnels and my people need not be so either. The things the factory had taught me as a Droneling fresh from the tank were designed to make me more useful to humanity, but did little to teach me about my own people. It wasn't that I wanted to be as humans were, only that I had potential beyond what a single-minded AI in the factory had told me.

The moment I put my hand in the stream, the forest taught me I could be so much more than just Ezra One, Drone of Under-district 00154. I never told anyone because I was afraid people would laugh or think I was grasping at intangible things that weren't really there. The nice thing about that experience, I needed it to be validated by no one, because it validated me.

I spent the next few hours wandering the woods lost in thought, something I'd had little time for in the last seventy-two hours, let alone in my entire life. There was a moment when I wanted to just disappear into the woods and seek my destiny elsewhere. That feeling was fleeting as my devotion to my friends and my own unwillingness to run from my problems won out.

I went back to the cabin and found Taylor and Silverstein sitting outside, sharing a cigarette. Silverstein raised his hand to greet me as I walked up the hill. Taylor gave me an odd look. I wondered if she could see the metamorphosis I'd undergone somehow, if I was really that transparent.

"Ezra, you're all muddy, what have you been doing?" She giggled as she pointed at my dirty boots and trousers.

"Nothing, just making sure this location is secure," I reported.

Taylor nodded approvingly, probably seeing right through me. Silverstein ground out the cigarette and handed me a small daypack. Then Taylor and I took the seat behind him in the four-wheeled vehicle.

"The CGG's server farms aren't far from here, we should be able to make it on the charge in this vehicle. I pulled the battery from the other one just in case," he said.

The vehicle rolled along silently beneath us as the sky began to darken. I was glad we chose to approach the area by night, preferring the cover of darkness. I hoped to get a glimpse of Finland by night as well, maybe even walk in the woods again.

We parked about a mile from the server farm complex and hid our vehicle beneath fallen brush. I was able to see in the dark merely by removing my goggles, something I wondered about. It seems silly now that I assumed they only worked in the tunnels and downtown Port Montaigne. More lies revealed for the fiction they were.

I could see the high chain link fence in the distance, a few spotlights, and what I assumed to be a few cooking fires. The smell was all wrong though, and I started getting a sinking feeling. Passing through the final copse, the front gate was visible. I gasped at the sight arrayed before me, prompting Silverstein and Taylor to lower themselves to the ground.

"The gate house is smoldering and the guards are laying dead amidst what look like a hundred or so spent shell casings. I can see where a large tracked vehicle rolled over the top of one. Whatever it was, it was wider than the gate," I reported softly.

Silverstein sank lower onto the ground and closed his eyes for a moment while Taylor strained over my shoulder to get a glimpse. Looking further up I could see there were a few more plumes of smoke reaching up toward the sky. From what I could see, they probably weren't cooking fires.

"We still have to go in there," Silverstein concluded.

I reached into the pack and withdrew a web belt that displayed several knives, a short range radio, and a pair of shaped explosives. Strapping it on, I swapped my dim set of goggles for my clear ones and tucked my trousers into my boots. I clicked a pair of vambraces onto my wrists Matthias had laying around.

Taylor and Silverstein made their own preparations, then we walked out skirting the outside of the chain link fence. We walked past nearly a dozen dead members of the Finnish army and a couple of smoldering vehicles and check points. Once we reached the base of the butte, I cut through the fence and we entered the grounds.

Gazing up, I could see the mountainside entrance, its large vault-like doors laying on their sides, the interior open to the frigid air. Wasting no time we made our way quickly through the first falling snow I'd seen so far to the opening. The interior was paneled in metal, and industrial-grade causeway. The no-slip surface of the floor had been marred by what was obviously a large, tracked vehicle.

I could smell the wretched thing in the air, heavy gauge wire, nuclear powered, and if the cyborgs I'd already encountered were any indication, manufactured by Madmar. I related what I smelled to Silverstein and Taylor whose faces mirrored my own apprehension. We were not properly prepared for this.

We walked to the first intersection, the frigid arctic wind howling at our backs. Looking to the right we could see a corridor that went down, then veered to the left. Looking to the right we could see pair of untouched blast doors not far away, still locked up tight. Straight ahead there was a heavy industrial elevator large enough to have born whatever metal monstrosity had torn its way in here.

In the end, we opted for the elevator. If anyone knew where they were going, Madmar probably did, and he had to be stopped.

CHAPTER 13

Somewhere in the permanent ice of the Canadian Arctic territory.

10:01 AM, December 31st, 2199

Log 01, Matthias Ericsson

"Pilot, we are arriving on site," the SA-C Aquiline AI reported.

"Scan for life," Matthias whispered as the armor set down on the arctic tundra.

The combat suit's sensor array penetrated the ground and ice easily bringing up a full three dimensional rendering of the massive facility below. The onboard AI quickly indicated that there were several hundred life forms concentrated in two sectors, both designated as factory units for metasapients.

"No human life signs detected."

Matthias pondered the readings. He was certain that Madmar had been using this facility, and maybe he had. The only way to know for certain was to gain access and look for clues of his passing.

"Metasapient types?" Matthias inquired.

"Acrididae and Chiroptera types detected," the SA-C Aquiline AI reported.

Matthias winced. Acrididae types were Metasapients fashioned from locust and human genetic material while the Chiroptera were crafted of human and bat DNA. They were extremely dangerous, and if unleashed without proper indoctrination, feral and potentially uncontrollable.

"Are the Metasapient life signals currently in stasis?" Matthias inquired.

"Affirmative."

Matthias crunched across the frozen ground sending out a signal to one of the landing bays to open. The ground suddenly split apart sending up a geyser of trapped air and debris as the huge loading doors slowly opened. They revealed a circular landing platform suitable for a medium sized transport.

Using the suit's jump jets to slowly descend, Matthias entered the landing area sending out a request for service. The bay doors slowly closed and several small automated servitors arrived to service the waiting vessel. They beeped to one another in confusion as there was no ship waiting for them.

The small automatons floated over to the suit of armor looking for joints or flight machinery to service. Matthias turned back the tinted visor on his suit and smiled at the whimsical semi-sentient devices. They each waved a greeting with their mechanical appendages.

"Fetch the Deck Sergeant or Master Technician please," Matthias asked over the suit's P.A.

"We cannot," the small machines chirped in unison.

"Explain," Matthias replied.

"He and she are both deactivated," the small machines chirped sadly.

Matthias had expected as much, but the base's AI still seemed to function properly. The small service machines suddenly departed back to their holding compartments along the perimeter of the landing area. The overhead lights dimmed suddenly plunging the whole area in darkness, then returned to normal a few moments later.

"Power fluctuations. Analyze the power network native to the complex for damage," Matthias whispered.

"Generators Alpha, Sigma, and Omega are offline."

"Scan for biological and nanotechnological agents and verify that nano-tech countermeasures are still in place," Matthias ordered, somewhat frantic.

"Classified Agent NT003 detected but dormant, all seals operating normally."

Matthias gritted his teeth. Madmar had dispersed a nanotechnological agent designed to invade the bodies of, and remotely control, everyone inside the complex. This control is permanent as the nano-machines would irreparably damage the brain to garner that control. The NT003 project had been shelved because the tiny machines would seek out energy sources toward the end of their life cycle damaging critical power systems in their dispersal radius. Not always an optimal outcome, even by the CGG's standards.

The Aquiline power armor carried Matthias silently over to the bay doors reacting to his movement in perfect sync. He reached out with both gauntlet-clad hands and leaned into the blast doors, forcing them apart slowly. Dust and a half-frozen hand dropped across the threshold.

Just inside were a pair of poor souls, starved to death. Matthias knelt down beside them, his armor sweeping the corridor for movement. They'd been dead a long time, the dust on them an inch thick.

Standing up, he had his suit power up its illuminators, casting a faint glow on the corridor. No one had walked through here in a very long time. The steel corridor was dark and deathly silent. Not even the hum of electrical conduit or hiss of hydraulic pressure broke the silence.

"Why would Madmar kill all these people and abandon a perfectly good hiding place?" Matthias said aloud.

"Insufficient data, query invalid," the SA-C Aquiline AI intoned.

The AI wasn't wrong, and Matthias knew it. There wasn't likely to be a trail of breadcrumbs in this place that would lead to Madmar, only more evidence of his madness. The corridor ended in more blast doors, these slightly ajar.

Matthias leaned into the doors, pushing into an interior chamber. He looked about the storage facility at unopened food rations, and the bodies of several people who starved to death a few feet away. None of the supplies appeared to be missing, even the valuable goods.

The living quarters beyond weren't that different. Men and women, working for the CGG's military and research division, controlled and left to die by a madman for reasons apparent only to him.

The science and robotics sector was filled with people suspended in tubes of fluid. Each had machinery painfully invading their craniums and implanted with a neural interface that allowed them to control a piece of hardware remotely. Matthias couldn't be sure what exactly, and none of them was alive to ask.

One man in particular wasn't merely cut from life support. Someone had, in gruesome fashion, tortured the man to death. Judging by his hands, he worked for a living previous to being pressed into whatever grisly service Madmar had required of him. Matthias could only wonder what he could have possibly done to deserve such a fate. How they got down here and for how long was to remain a mystery. All systems were dormant.

He reached the Acrididae manufacturing wing finding it fully powered. The doors opened easily with his old passcode and he entered still suited up. Everything inside seemed intact, the Metasapients tucked safely into their stasis pods.

The M-Unit, a complex AI designed to teach the Metasapients their role in society when they are released from stasis, appeared to be operating normally on auxiliary power. Matthias walked up to the control interface at the center of the manufacturing floor. The panel illuminated at his approach.

"Hello, Matthias," said a voice from the M-Unit.

"Madmar," Matthias replied, gazing down at the display on the M-Unit.

"Aquiline Jump Trooper armor, very nice! You might need it soon," Madmar replied via the remote feed.

"We need to finish this. Tell me when and where," Matthias said.

"Oh, there will be no epic final confrontation between us. I know with perfect knowledge I'm no match for you. You're a Mechanic, a tele-mechanic psychic, you'd kill me without breaking a sweat in that armor. That was your plan, right?" Madmar said, laughing.

"Madmar, what have you done?"

Orange lights began to flash around the manufacturing facility as two sets of blast doors closed at each entrance. Matthias looked about as fluid began to drain from the stasis chambers. One by one, Acrididae Metasapients began waking up as the M-Unit powered down.

"Our mutual friends will wake up and see to you while I make sure Taylor and her allies are put to proper use in Finland," Madmar said.

"This isn't over, Madmar," Matthias said.

"Oh, I think it is," he replied.

The Metasapients exited their chambers and slowly made their way toward where Matthias stood. The Acrididae were designed for heavy manufacturing and military operations, and were strong enough to bite through steel. Against one hundred of them, no one was likely to survive.

Matthias lowered his head as the lights went out, Madmar's fading voice blotted out by the chittering and scuttling of the hungry Acrididae.

CHAPTER 14

Uptown, Port Montaigne - Doc's Tavern

7:12 PM, February 13th, 2159 – 40 years prior to shutdown.

It wasn't much of a bar, and it didn't look like there was kitchen. Ashton shook the rain off and headed over to the table in the back marked 'Reserved'. Unlike the rest of the dingy establishment, the booth was clean and still smelling of disinfectant. The seat creaked as he sat down, the faux leather grabbing at this pant legs as he slid toward the wall.

There wasn't much on the wall except a sign behind the bar saying "Established, 2017." Everything in the bar was old including the cash register, bar stools, and the flickering flat panel TV silently displaying college basketball highlights. Ashton could remember going into places like this with his grandfather for Rotary meetings when he was a kid.

He was hungry as hell, so he grabbed a menu from the next table over. The waitress brought over two glasses of water, dropping them off with two coasters. When Ashton looked up from the table to order, she was already gone.

The door opened a moment later, the torrential rain framing a single man as he came inside and shook off an umbrella with a wooden handle and dark blue parasol. He was tall and thin, dressed in what looked like vintage clothing from the last century and a well-made coffee colored leather jacket. Ashton couldn't help but notice his shoes. They were worth more than the rest of his outfit combined.

The man hung his jacket by the door like he'd done so a million times, then nodded to the barkeep and walked straight back. He lingered beside the booth where Ashton was sitting for a moment, and then sat down across from him. There was an awkward silence as Ashton watched him pull out what looked like an antique cigarette from his shirt pocket and lit it.

"Didn't think you could even buy those things on this continent," Ashton said, looking around nervously.

"You can't, and do relax. We're just going to have a nice chat," the man said, waving the waitress over.

She came over and dropped off what was probably the only ashtray in Port Montaigne.

"Are you Vance? Am I sitting with the right man here?" Ashton asked.

"Yeah, thanks for coming to meet me. Sorry about all the cloak and dagger, but I like to keep a low profile," Vance said with a nod and a smile, waving the smoke from his face.

"I figured it might be like this eventually," Ashton said.

"Like what?" Vance asked.

"I've got the only company trying to produce commercial and consumer grade intelligent agents. The brand new Central Global Government has passed judgment saying artificial intelligence is only safe when used with military or governmental operational safeguards. For months now, someone has been helping me stay afloat from the shadows. Every time I meet the mysterious investor it turns out he's just an errand boy bringing me another tip or infusion of credit. Are you the guy, or just another courier?" Ashton said, his stomach growling loudly.

"Hungry?" Vance asked, crushing what remained of his cigarette into the ashtray.

"You had me riding trains and walking through empty parking garages for hours to get here, what do you think?" Ashton said, shaking his head and smiling in disbelief.

"You okay to walk in the rain? I know a place that's got pretty good food," Vance said, standing up.

The waitress brought over his coat, which Vance exchanged for an envelope.

"Yeah, why not," Ashton said shaking his head.

Ashton followed Vance through the back out into the alley. The buildings of uptown Port Montaigne cast a long shadow over the west side as they walked back out to the street. They crossed the block as ancient cars crawled past toward the outskirts and the suburbs beyond, the last trickle of commuters gone for the day.

They entered an old office building that had been converted into apartments. There were dusty signs saying that they would be taking renters soon, but Ashton doubted they would be. The whole place was empty and smelled of fresh paint and caulking. After a short flight of metal stairs, and another hallway, Vance pulled out some keys and unlocked an apartment door.

"I thought we were getting something to eat?" Ashton said, looking around nervously.

Vance nodded and headed into the apartment. Ashton cursed and followed him into what could have been a tastefully upholstered apartment. There was little in the way of furniture except for a desk and a kitchen table. Across every wall and surface there were stacks of paper, print outs, and file folders, relics of a by-gone era. Virtually no one used paper anymore, and a lot of what was in the room had yellowing edges indicating that the paper was old.

"I got takeout earlier, it'll just take a minute to heat it up. There's a coat closet by the front door if you want to hang up your coat," Vance said, walking into the kitchen.

"You're the guy? Not a courier, not an errand boy, and not a friend of a friend of a friend?" Ashton said, looking around somewhat surprised.

"Yeah, I'm the guy. Sit wherever you'd like," Vance said, pulling a couple of white take-out containers from the fridge and sliding them into an ancient looking microwave.

Ashton shrugged, already completely bewildered, and sat down at the table mostly obscured by stacks of paper. He looked over at Vance, his mind going a million miles per hour. Vance looked like he couldn't be more than twenty-five. He was a lot different than the room full of old white men smoking flavored e-cigars Ashton suspected he'd find once he was allowed to finally meet with his mysterious investors.

"You can just set that stuff on the floor. I'm getting ready to have most of it incinerated after you and I talk. You cool with chopsticks? " Vance said, bringing two plates of Thai food over.

"Yeah, that's fine," Ashton said, clearing them a space on the table.

"I guess you'd like to know why I've been investing in your company," Vance said,

Ashton glanced at the papers he was setting on the floor. It looked like financial records from a dozen different holding companies and banks. It was accounting mumbo-jumbo that was far out of his depth of experience and dangerous information to just leave lying around.

"I'm a little curious, yeah. All your representatives said that I was the only one you'd work with. There are plenty of companies sitting under the umbrella of the CGG's military and government contracts. All legal, publicly traded and profitable," Ashton said, folding his arms.

Vance nodded and smiled.

"Matthias Ericsson, your intern, he needs to stay on board and take a greater role in intelligent agent development," Vance said, taking a bite.

"He's a gifted programmer. Keeping him onboard won't be a problem. He a relative of yours or something?" Ashton said, poking around in his food.

"Matthias and I have never met, and God willing, we never will. It's better for everyone involved if this is that last time we meet directly and you deny having every seen me to anyone who asks," Vance said handing Ashton a soda.

"Look, I'll keep him around, but he rubs everyone the wrong way. He's convinced that intelligent agents will break down and become unstable if they don't have a strong integrated sense of morality. No one else thinks that's going to be commercially viable," Ashton said, opening the soda.

"Not good enough. As soon as he's deep enough in your company, put him in charge of his own project and give me weekly progress reports. The other guys you've got on staff just want to make a paycheck. Matthias wants to make something important," Vance said, locking eyes with Ashton.

Ashton looked into the young man's eyes and saw something he'd only ever seen in two people, his grandfather, and the man who gave him his first real job delivering appliances in college. Vance had more than just an old soul, but an unwavering certitude in what he was doing. It was clear now this wasn't about money or profit, it was about something else.

"Yeah, okay, whatever you want. You want to tell me why this is so important to you?" Ashton asked, throwing up his hands.

"You're thirty-five and married, right? Got kids?" Vance said without malice, sounding genuinely curious to hear Ashton's reply.

"I think you probably know I do," Ashton replied.

"Intelligent agents are just like your kids. They need to be taught, shown the difference between right and wrong, and protected from the people who would harm them," Vance explained.

"You think someone is really going to do it, don't you? No one believes we're even close to creating a thinking machine with the capacity to learn and feel like a human being. Even the most senior programmers at the biggest firms know it is all marketing and hype. There is no bright future where the thinking machine works side by side its human creator, not any time soon anyway," Ashton said, doing his best to be honest.

"It's already happened," Vance said, pulling another cigarette out from his shirt pocket.

Ashton was baffled.

"I think a Nobel Prize would have been handed out if someone had pulled it off," Ashton said holding up his hands and shaking his head.

"I won't burden you with the specifics, but there are at least two active artificial intelligences," Vance said, heading to the kitchen for seconds. "Both of them are controlled by our new global government. Scientists working at the CGG and private companies with contracts are trying to replicate the process of creating similarly complex intelligent agents."

"Thanks, I really don't want to know the specifics. Knowing and distributing that information without the right security clearance could land you in prison for the rest of your life. Why would you risk telling me any of this?" Ashton asked, setting the chopsticks down.

"If regular people are going to have a chance of maintaining a say in their government and control over their destiny, they need equal access to the same sort of technology," he replied, sitting back down with a full plate.

"I agree, but if you're right and my company has the potential to produce a viable intelligent agent, what's to stop the government from swooping in and taking it out from underneath me? All they have to do is declare my holdings necessary to the 'global civic order' and assign someone they can control to take over. I'll be out, and they'll have a third intelligent agent," Ashton asked, suddenly not hungry anymore.

"You took my money and kept right on moving, hardly giving a thought about who I was or what I was about. There are a lot of people in the government that are exactly the same. They just want to go to work, collect a paycheck, and go home to their families at the end of the day. I know you don't care whether the next intelligent agent brought into our world has a conscience, but I do," Vance said, standing up from the table, taking Ashton's plate.

"This is crazy," Ashton said, taking a sip of his soda, hoping the bubbles would quell his troubled stomach.

"I brought you here to let you know what's on the line and how important it is to me. To take it a step further, I don't believe that the government is colluding with those two intelligent agents to undermine the public. Personally, I think they're more like lost children being held hostage by a gang of unscrupulous thugs," Vance said, putting the dishes in the sink.

"You're serious? And, you think I'm just in this for the money?" Ashton asked.

"Aren't you?" Vance said, putting his hands up behind his head and leaning back in the chair.

"Honestly, I don't know anymore."

"Remember the kid trapped in a closet last year? She made that impassioned plea for rescue? It went viral all over the world and had law enforcement in two dozen countries and provinces looking for her." Vance put his hands down on the table in front of him.

"Yeah, it was a rich kid at the lunar resort using a modified data slate and a program she downloaded from the Internet to make it look like she was calling from a half dozen places back on Earth. CGG passed all kinds of new regulations to prevent something like that happening again."

"The child was real, and the closet she'd was locked in was the Central Lunar Mainframe. The call was made by an intelligent agent that was confused, scared, and being kept in a dark place," Vance said quietly.

Ashton sat and thought for a moment. There were a lot of things about the cellular call made by the child that didn't add up. It saturated the media and everyone could pretty much recite what she'd said, word for word now. When the dispatcher asked where her parents were, she wasn't sure she'd ever had any. The real kid's identity was never leaked to the media in the aftermath, a virtual impossibility given how fluidly information traveled through the Internet.

"They aren't like real kids, Vance. They're artificial and they don't--"

Vance banged his fist on the table, startling Ashton.

"You didn't even believe they could exist before talking to me. Don't assume to know more about it than I do. The intelligent agent that made that phone call are not any less real than your own kids!" Vance yelled, his eyes narrowing.

"Yeah, okay, but what do you want me to do about it? You're talking about taking on a global conspiracy perpetrated by people at the highest levels of government," Ashton said, holding up his hands.

"Just what I told you. I want Matthias at the head of his own project, full creative license, and weekly progress reports," he said, looking away from Ashton, and rubbing his hands together anxiously.

"I can do that, but he's just a kid. I'm not sure what makes you think he'll be the one to break through the creative wall that's kept everyone else from producing a true and stable intelligent agent," Ashton said, holding his gut.

"I'm a long term planner and thinker. I'm not expecting results next week, or even next year. I didn't come this far without learning to be very patient," Vance said, resuming his previous cool.

"I thought when I finally met my principle investor, things would go a little differently," Ashton said, shaking his head.

"Me, too," Vance replied.

"Okay, let's assume what you're saying is true. How is having your own intelligent agent going to help?" Ashton asked.

"The two intelligent agents the CGG have managed to create or steal are unstable, they'll become corrupt and terminate within a few years. The intelligent agents I want to see created will not suffer that fate. What's more, I don't intend to 'own' him, her, or it. Slavery is illegal, and the CGG is breaking their own laws by holding and using the two intelligent agents they already have," Vance replied, taking a bite of food.

"Right, okay, but I still don't see how you intend to take on a global organization tasked with governance over us all," Ashton said, pulling out a bottle of pills.

"Pray you never do."

CHAPTER 15

Somewhere near Helsinki, Finland

9:36 PM, December 30th, 2199

Taylor peaked around the corner, looking past a case of server components. The underground chamber of the CGG's server farm was like a multi-level hockey rink. Layers of ice and industrial fans worked to keep the various layers frigid.

Silverstein and Ezra shivered in the cold as they made their way down the underground tunnel to where Taylor waited. She nodded, pointing her thumb back over her shoulder. Quietly, they took up positions next to her and gazed down the causeway at what she'd found.

"It's huge," Silverstein said.

"It's an Eclipse Class rover, designed for heavy gravity hostile environments. Before the manufacturing facility released me, I was taught to use one. Never had the chance to use one again," Ezra said.

The huge tracked vehicle sat at the right hand side of the corridor beside a row of servers covered in a layer of frost. The top of the massive vehicle barely made it below the sheet of ice suspended above. It had already destroyed an array of industrial fans as it made its way through to the first set of server banks.

The Eclipse was a tracked vehicle equipped with two heavy robot arms and festooned with weapons. It was sheathed in heavy armor plating with only a small ten inch diameter porthole allowing the pilot visual access to the outside. To compensate, the vehicle was covered in micro-cameras and sensors.

"Stay here," Ezra said.

"You can't go out there, that thing will kill you," Silverstein said, grabbing Ezra by the arm.

"You guys have to get to the servers so you can do what you do. Maybe I can get this thing to follow me so you can get past. At this stage, what happens to me doesn't matter," Ezra whispered, pulling away.

"It matters to us, so be careful," Silverstein said.

Taylor and Silverstein watched as Ezra crept down the corridor, stepping over the ice shattered in the rover's wake. The vehicle didn't move, even as Ezra crawled on all fours up beside it. Taylor grabbed Silverstein's hand tightly in the tense moments after Ezra disappeared around the front of the rover.

Moments later, Ezra reappeared, waving them over. Taylor and Silverstein walked carefully over to where Ezra stood and gazed down at the floor in front of the rover. A neat hole had been cut into the almost thirty inch thick ice beneath them.

Silverstein gave the rover a quick look. No pilot. The front had seen some action though, it's armored hide pockmarked by gunfire.

The hold went to a lower level where many more server banks could be dimly seen. Taylor turned to Silverstein and Ezra who looked to the causeway ahead. Like her, they weren't sure if they should go down or continue further toward the core.

"Someone cut this hole for a purpose. One of Madmar's agents, perhaps?" Ezra sniffed the air.

"They might know where they're going better than we do. They'll need to be stopped regardless," Silverstein concluded.

Ezra dropped through the gap first, then Taylor, and finally Silverstein, landing roughly on the icy floor below. The hum of the industrial fans drowned out all other sounds as Ezra ran his small hand across the floor. He nodded to his comrades and pointed down the corridor.

They followed the intruder's trail through the icy tunnels and past hundreds of server banks. The corridors were wide, dark save a few indicator lights from the hardware arrayed around them, and clouded by a perpetual haze.

Finally they came upon a circular bank of servers that seemed to sit at the center of all the others. Dozens of corridors radiated off from this area. A lone figure stood near the only terminal access to the core server bank.

The trio froze in their tracks, trying to get a better look at the person they'd been tracking for the last hour. He wore winter clothes, a dark cold weather jacket, and fur-lined boots. He stood there as if waiting for something, hands in his pockets.

"He's waiting for us," Ezra whispered.

"Could be," Taylor said.

The man turned to face them, his countenance dimly illuminated by a data slate held in his right hand. He had every appearance of being a young man save his white hair and cold eyes. Taking down the hood on his coat, the man beckoned to the trio.

"Come on, we should get this over with," he said plainly.

Startled, Silverstein approached slowly, Taylor and Ezra pacing off wide to either side. The man was sporting a few days of stubble and his eyes were tired. His gaze did not waiver from his data slate as he spoke.

"Dr. Maurice Madmar, I presume," Silverstein said.

"Vance Uroboros I've met before, and you must be Taylor and Ezra One."

Silverstein bristled at the use of his own name.

"Whatever it is you came here to do, we're going to stop you," Silverstein said.

"I've already had to drastically alter my plans because of you, Vance. You're hiding of the financial resources in the world, locking it into funds that won't mature in our lifetime while letting the bank borrow against their own debt. My efforts to control the world by replacing key persons with my synthetic replicas seems cliché by comparison," Madmar mused.

"Why would I have done such a thing?" Silverstein questioned.

"Really, it's the only thing I hadn't considered, and one of only a handful of ways I could have been stopped," Madmar said, still staring at the data slate.

"More lies to cover up the other ones?" Taylor taunted.

Madmar smiled broadly and looked up from his data slate. His cold eyes settled on Taylor.

"The Terrestrial AI, daughter of the two Lunar AIs. A matched set designed to preserve humanity in the wake of any potential catastrophe on earth. The Two created a handful of children to experience what it is to be human," Madmar said.

Ezra lunged forward, his claws extended.

"Hold it!" Madmar yelled.

Ezra froze, a look of consternation coming across his face.

"That's right. You will find it difficult to attack anyone with my vocal signature. When my colleagues and I designed the Drones, we made sure there were some certain countermeasures in place so they'd be easy to control," Madmar cackled.

Ezra blinked sadly for a moment, then delivered a savage blow to Madmar's throat. Madmar went down hard, his data slate clattering to the floor. He looked up in surprise as Ezra's small form loomed over him.

"Throat implant, designed to make you sound like an M-Unit? That was your plan to keep me from tearing you limb from limb?" Ezra sneered.

Ezra kicked Madmar, sending him sliding across the floor. He came painfully to rest against the core server bank. The tiny Drone reached down slowly, picking up Madmar's data slate. He handed it off to Silverstein.

"How--?" Madmar coughed.

"Consider this my resignation. I'm not a Drone or Ezra One anymore, just Ezra. Just. Ezra," he growled, pointing his clawed finger at Madmar.

"Wow, that was awesome," Taylor said, clasping her hands together.

Silverstein looked at the data slate, squinting as he tried to make sense of what he saw. Silverstein ran over to the core server interface and tapped on the input screen. It lit up, prompting him for identification.

"What? What is it?" Taylor asked.

"Madmar's already dropped code to the servers that will prompt an audit of CGG's financials. If it completes, it'll cause a cascade of foreclosures pushing millions of people out of their homes, businesses and government buildings. Total shutdown," Silverstein muttered as he began trying to access the server.

"It's too late, Vance. I injected the code almost an hour ago. Hospitals, government run retirement homes, clinics, courthouses, subsidized housing... all shuttered. Automated systems will expel their occupants out into the cold. Even if they manage to get back inside, there will be no power, water, heat, or services," Madmar rasped, clutching his ribs.

Silverstein's fingers tapped furiously across the interface screen bringing up screen after screen. All the welfare countermeasures were offline and the backups were deleted. Even worse, all the automated buildings, particularly those with the capability, were authorized to use lethal force in evicting occupants. Even with archaic heavy equipment that was off the grid, some of these buildings would be completely inaccessible. Vehicles both commercial and military that relied on the CGG mainframe would cease to function and fall from the sky. Even the most peaceful countries would tear themselves apart as people struggled to simply survive.

Silverstein backed away from the input panel and turned his gaze to Madmar. Ezra grabbed him up by his lapels and held him up to the input panel. The strong Drone leaned into Madmar, his clawed hand wrapped tightly around his throat.

"It's really him, not a synthetic replica," Ezra whispered, turning his nose up at Madmar.

"I can't get the servers to respond. It's still directing all its resources to performing the audit," Silverstein said.

"Let me try," Taylor said.

Silverstein stepped aside, letting Taylor take his place at the input panel. She placed her hands on around the edges of the panel allowing the screen go dark, almost cradling the interface. She entwined her fingers in the plethora of cords leading up to the precipice where she stood and closed her eyes.

The servers all suddenly beeped in unison, the fans cooling them slowing for a moment. Ezra dragged Madmar away from the server core as he struggled. Silverstein watched as the indicators on the servers around the core went from red to green.

"Madmar lied," Taylor whispered, her eyes still closed.

"About what?" Silverstein said looking on somewhat mystified.

"I wasn't sent here to learn about human beings. I was sent here to save as many as I can," Taylor said.

"Can you stop or undo what Madmar and I have done?"

"What you did under the alias of 'Uroboros' bears only a passing similarity to what Madmar claimed. He's tried to rob you of your dignity in the same way you robbed him of financial and political control of more than sixty percent of the countries on the CGG's grid," Taylor intoned.

"Taylor, you still there? You don't sound like yourself," Silverstein said putting his hand on her shoulder.

Taylor smiled.

"My mother and father sent me to find you and watch over you, but something went wrong. Even being bereft of knowing my function, I still managed to fulfil it. I was drawn to you even when we both didn't know the truth of ourselves. Do you think we met by coincidence?" Taylor said.

"Sort of," Silverstein remarked sadly.

"I can't save them all. So much of what Madmar has done cannot be undone. Many people will die, go hungry, or succumb to the cold. There are a few that will be spared because of our efforts."

Ezra clenched his teeth lifting Madmar over his head, then brought him back down on the ground hard. Madmar coughed as Ezra punched him over and over. Silverstein rushed over and tried to take Ezra by the wrist, getting thrown to the ground for his troubles.

"Ezra, stop! Stop!" Silverstein pleaded.

Madmar cackled through broken teeth and bloodied lips as Ezra backed off.

"He deserves to die for what he's done," Ezra hissed, pointing at Madmar.

"He was waiting for us," Silverstein shouted.

Ezra's rage quickly cooled as he looked around the server core.

"Why would he wait for us like this if there even a chance of us stopping him? What are you really up to, Madmar?" Silverstein shouted.

"I forget just how paranoid you really are, Uroboros," he cackled.

Silverstein ran back over to where Taylor was standing and looked down at the input panel. Taylor isolated systems within the CGG grid that would preserve power and services in different places. There was something else however, something terrible.

"Taylor, step down out of there. Get away from the input panel," Silverstein said.

"Even more people will die if I do," she replied.

"The more you expose your own programing to the grid, the more Madmar will know about you and the Lunar AIs. He may be out to ruin the Earth, but it's the moon he's really after."

"If I do, millions more will die. As the lights go off and transports stop running around the world, people will freeze, burn, and starve. I cannot abandon them," Taylor said, tears running down her cheeks, her hands trembling with fatigue.

"I understand. You can't. But, we can," Silverstein said nodding to Ezra.

Ezra and Silverstein grabbed Taylor and pulled her from the input panel. She struggled feebly as Silverstein pulled her away, his hands wrapped tightly around her waist. Ezra smashed the terminal, raking his claws across the wires and cables that connected it to the server core. Sparks flew as the core quickly overheated, bursting into flames.

"NO! I was so close!" Madmar cried out in anger as he stood and dashed down one of the corridors, disappearing into the mist. Ezra turned to give chase but halted as the ice above the central server cracked loudly. "We've got to get out of here!" Ezra cried out.

Silverstein grabbed up Taylor in his arms and ran like hell, following Ezra as fire quickly spread behind them. The ice that acted as support to so much of the core structure began to break. Up ahead, the rover had already crashed through making a convenient if not treacherous way back to the upper level.

Ezra grabbed Silverstein by the hand and helped him up to solid ground. Moments later, as they caught their breath, the entire server complex collapsed under its own weight, forcing smoke and fire upward. Ezra held out his arms, offering to carry Taylor the rest of the way.

"No, I got this," Silverstein said, looking down at Taylor as she lapsed in and out of consciousness.

They ran the last length of tunnel on adrenaline alone clearing the cave access and out into the open. Ezra stopped dead in his tracks, his ears straining to hear even the faintest sound. He could hear a transport taking off somewhere nearby, still operational.

"He's getting away," Ezra said.

"Let him, we need to get Taylor out of here," Silverstein said.

"Let's use the gate," Ezra said.

As they came upon fallen army personnel, Ezra stooped over and picked up their rifles. After checking for ammunition, he slung the still useful firearms over his shoulder and discarded the others. Silverstein followed, stopping to try and revive Taylor along the way.

They closed the distance to the front gate and slipped through to the other side. A hundred yards later, they broke into the woods in the pitch black of the night. Snow began to fall as they walked the last mile to where they hid the rover.

Ezra pulled the brush aside while Silverstein tried to, again, revive Taylor. She was cold, even more so than the Scandinavian wilderness around them. She'd pushed herself to the brink, accessing several hundred thousand computer systems at once in a not-quite-vain attempt to save as many people as she could.

"Ezra, I don't think she's okay," Silverstein said, sitting down in the snow.

"She has to be," Ezra said, kneeling down beside him.

"We need to get her back to the cabin."

"The cabin seems to be a place off the grid with a wood stove, food, and a well. Anyone who knows about it, is going to head for it," Ezra said.

"Could be, and we'll be totally out of power for the rover by the time we get there. What'll we do?" Silverstein asked, standing up.

"World's a changed place, we'll have to do our best to protect what's ours," Ezra said, loading one of the rifles.

"So, we go from saving the world, to merely trying to survive in it?" Silverstein said sadly.

Ezra nodded solemnly. "For now."

Silverstein gave a single nod, still numb from everything that had just happened. Laying Taylor in the back he took off his own coat and wrapped her in it. She stirred slightly, making Silverstein hesitate for a moment before climbing into the driver's seat.

They drove slowly with the headlights off. The open-topped vehicle bobbed back and forth over the rough road, its electric motor the only mechanical sound for miles. Even with Helsinki a few miles away, there wasn't a single transport in the sky and the early morning glow coming off the buildings at the horizon was gone.

The cabin was dark when they arrived. Ezra did a walk around before Silverstein parked. Ezra grabbed the guns and the batteries out of the rover while Silverstein carried Taylor. The inside of the cabin was cold, and Ezra was wary of building a fire.

"You look tired. I'll take the first watch," Ezra said, bringing one of the rifles up to his shoulder.

Silverstein nodded, laying down beside Taylor on the floor by the front door. Ezra stepped outside and vanished into the darkness. Taylor stirred as the door closed.

"Where are we?" Taylor whispered.

"We're at the cabin," Silverstein replied, breathing a sigh of relief.

"Why did you pull me away? I could have helped so many people."

"Aside from preventing Madmar getting access to the Lunar AIs and lording over us from the Lunar Colony?" he replied.

"I saw the virus, I was going to shut myself down before it got to me," Taylor replied.

"When you say shut down, you mean die, right?"

"My life, if I even count, in exchange for how many others?"

"You count," Silverstein said holding her closer.

"You still haven't answered my question. Why did you pull me away?"

"Back when we first met, I promised you I wouldn't let anything happen to you. I'd let the whole world go dark before I would break that promise."

Continued Book 2

Made in the USA
Coppell, TX
18 January 2021

48412136R00115